40P

CLA

The Qu

EAST SUSSEX COUNTY LIBRARY

WITHDRAWN

21 JAN 2002

77

COLLINS, 8 GRAFTON STREET, LONDON W1

William Collins Sons & Co. Ltd
London · Glasgow · Sydney · Auckland
Toronto · Johannesburg

EAST SUSSEX

V	D	INV No	0899
CLASS	F		
OK	126166		AZ
CAT	✓	DATE	

COUNTY LIBRARY

288795 ✓

First published 1986
© Clare Curzon 1986

British Library Cataloguing in Publication Data

Curzon, Clare
    The quest for K.—(Crime Club)
    I. Title
    823′.914[F]   PR6053.U7/

    ISBN 0 00 231429 0

Photoset in Linotron Baskerville by
Rowland Phototypesetting Ltd
Bury St Edmunds, Suffolk
Printed in Great Britain by
William Collins Sons & Co. Ltd, Glasgow

600 06

CHAPTER 1

The first time that Athens Flight OA269 showed on the Heathrow Arrivals Board it was already running late. Due in at 14.55 hours, the revised ETA was 17.15. Which meant time to kill for those waiting.

Detective-Inspector Angus Mott, casual in towelling sports shirt and jeans, ran a hand through his crisp, fair hair, rocked once on his crêpe soles and, a head taller than most, began to make his way through the crowd towards Terminal One. Over there coffee and a Danish tasted much the same but the view was richer. He settled himself in a lone chair opposite the glass wall and stared out at leisurely take-offs and landings, the caterpillar wanderings of trains of luggage trolleys stacked with suitcases; and quietly savoured activity which for once he was not obliged to be involved in, entertained by the giveaway body language of travellers. The nervous and the blasé; the hopeful and the furtive; the beloved and the bored; the fakes and the real McCoys: they were all streaming past. And a few moments later, with different faces and clothes the same mixture went by again, like a changing carousel.

A frizzy-haired waitress came on teetering heels to tell him that if he meant to eat he should be back among the tables. He had time to see the girl behind the pantomime-kitten make-up and showed her his broad melon-slice of square, white teeth. She swallowed the complaint, took his order, signalled back with dimples she'd worked hard on as a schoolgirl with the point of a lead pencil. Angus didn't miss her end-of-shift transfer of weight from ankle to tired ankle. She didn't have to strain her muscles with those killing heels, but if appearance meant so much and she liked herself that way, all right. His eyes told her he thought she looked good. She took his order and brought it promptly.

Overhead the clouds had cleared and the sky had gone a hazy, lazy blue. It would be a beautiful evening, perhaps a spectacular night. He allowed the professional part of himself to run finally down and switch off. As from noon today he was on a two-week leave, which would be the best ever, starting the moment Paula walked out from the Arrivals section.

At fifteen minutes off the new ETA he made his way back to Terminal Two. Her pilot might have caught up a little on schedule. Allow twenty-five minutes to get through Passport Control and Customs, then journey's end. Lovers' meeting. He hunched his broad shoulders, grinning warmly inside, walked over to the wall video.

Yet another ETA. Eighteen-fifty. Ah, well. Some things were worth waiting for.

At seventeen thirty-two Flight OA269 went right off the screen. The following numbers flicked smartly upwards to fill in the gap.

Mott stared at the list, read it through again. Some flights already showed the sign 'landed'. There was no OA269 any more. Not even a 'delayed' entry. He waited, suspecting a careless hand on the keyboard. In a moment the omission would be corrected.

Some four minutes later there was a new showing on the video without any ETA. *For Flight OA269 see BA Inquiries.* He knew then with a sick lurch of apprehension that this was only the beginning.

At BA Inquiries they'd no idea what he was asking about. A pert redhead in uniform swivelled a printed card and read off the printed schedule for him. He demurred and she did a double-take, frowned, punched a computer keyboard. The display told her to consult BA Inquiries. She *was* BA Inquiries, and she hadn't a clue.

A query to a passing airline official and then a phone call

followed. By now a dozen or more people were waiting in a fuming queue.

'Right, right,' the girl said into the receiver. She was waving her fingers as if drying nail enamel. 'Sorry,' she told Angus, and her eyelids fluttered to include the others behind him. 'OA269 has been diverted to Frankfurt. Some passengers may be distributed to other flights. For the rest it may mean further delay, I'm afraid. Sorry.'

'Which other flights?' Angus demanded, and over his shoulder a dark-skinned woman asked, 'But why? What is happening?'

'Technical trouble,' the girl temporized. 'Either they'll fix the trouble on the spot and come in later, or we'll be sending out a relief plane to bring them back.'

'Relief?' a man said cynically. 'Like you've got an odd Airbus standing around unused? In mid-season? With all regular services overbooked as it is? You'll have to think up a better one, miss.'

'We'll let you know the flight details when they come through,' the girl said doggedly. Her programming was getting worn at the edges. She tried the personal approach. 'It's Frankfurt, you see, so it rests with Lufthansa now as host country. They make the decisions and take over the passenger list. Just as we carry the can at this end.'

'She can't give us any more yet,' Angus told the others. 'We have to wait.' He turned back to her. 'How long d'you think, before there's something definite?'

'Half an hour. Better make that three-quarters. Something should be through by then.'

Reluctantly the little crowd dispersed. Angus remained conscious of them sunk on benches or dejectedly standing where scheduled passengers had to weave purposefully through them towards Departures. The scene was strangely familiar and the recognition chilled him. They had the stunned, washed-up air of crash survivors. Disasters were common enough in his job, but this was something else.

Journey's End, wasn't it? Having Paula back, to himself, after her lone-girl holiday booked before ever they'd met. This was to be the beginning of their sailing fortnight together. Maybe the start of much more. And already there were hang-ups. It didn't augur well.

He moved away among the kiosks and bought a paper-back novel which he soon discovered he would never read. The first three pages were alien. After them he idly sampled the first paragraph and last page of each chapter. That way it gained pace and a taut enigmatic quality the author couldn't have hoped for. By the end of it he still had thirteen minutes to go, so he leaned back with eyes closed and supplied for himself the intervening plot. Readers' Indigest, he thought sourly, and dropped the book on an empty bench as he passed.

Back at BA Inquiries a more experienced official had taken over, efficient and very calm. She was talking to the dark-skinned woman of the first queue. The woman's troubled face suddenly relaxed and she nodded, hugging her arms across her chest. 'In the VIP Lounge, yes?' she checked. 'I wait and someone bring her?'

'That's right, Mrs Tsampos. Flight LH036 is due in at twenty-one hours, so she should be with you about ten minutes later. A stewardess will bring her through directly.'

'*Efkharistó polí!* Good, good! My little Tina a VIP, yes.'

'Miss Paula Musto,' Angus told the desk clerk. 'Have you anything on her?'

'We have only six passengers going through tonight,' she confided. 'Three minors travelling alone, two invalids and one Euro MP. Her name's not among those. Musto. Ah, here she is—boarded at Athens en route from Iraklion, Crete, now staying overnight at the Hotel Bristol, Frankfurt. She will be boarding a mid-morning flight tomorrow. Would you mind ringing in after nine a.m. for her flight details? Use the number on this card. We are very sorry, of course, about the inconvenience.'

'What actually happened? An attempted hijack?'

'Oh goodness, no.' She lowered her voice. 'A minor fault. The pilot put down at Stuttgart for an adjustment, took off and got an unsatisfactory reading again. So he made for Frankfurt because there's more room there and a better alternative service. That sort of thing can happen at any time. They're a good airline, first-rate pilots. Nothing at all to worry about.'

Except not having Paula back. Angus thanked the girl and turned away. Back in his car the sheaf of long-stemmed pink roses looked dejected in its Cellophane wrapping. He had an air timetable in the glove compartment and he ran a finger down the next morning's departures from Frankfurt. There were two BA flights and one Lufthansa listed for London. And there was still a chance of the original Airbus 300 being serviceable by tomorrow, or of a substitute being sent out. Why then did he have this deadly sense of calamity?

Because expectation had had him on a high, he supposed, and this was reaction. So how deflated and weary would Paula be now, on her way since leaving her hotel in Crete at breakfast-time? Poor love, he'd find out the Frankfurt hotel's number and give her a ring right now.

But even as Telecom Inquiries were chasing up the number he changed his mind. She had a right to her undisturbed dinner, bath or sleep. A telegram would be better. *No fuss* was the way she liked things. So, play it cool. *Hard luck Honeypot shall meet all flights tomorrow love Angus*.

She would read it and smile, tuck it in her handbag, know he'd be there waiting. And there would still be their first greetings left to say, once she was safely home.

He drove back to his flat in Reading which had been slicked into an unnatural state of tidiness by Mrs Forster's imperfectionist attentions. His travel case, ready packed and strapped, mocked him from inside the entrance, the overnight bag empty beside it. He went straight through to the kitchen and took a can of beer from the fridge, tore at the ring and downed half the contents in a gulp, more from petulance than thirst. Two bottles of Sancerre stood on the floor nearby, put ready for supper. He'd planned the meal and half prepared it himself. Now that was all for nothing.

More slowly he finished the beer, leaning in the doorway of the bedroom, and recalled ordering fresh linen, hopeful that he wouldn't be obliged to use the single bed in the spare room himself. But just in case, he'd had that made up too, risking Mrs Forster's single smothered snort of disbelief. The choice was up to Paula; had been. He supposed that now they would travel tomorrow straight from Heathrow to Chichester harbour and go aboard, stopping off on the way for lunch at some pub that took their fancy. And on the ketch Barry Newell and his blonde wife Angie already installed in the double cabin. Singles for Paula and himself. In view of how things had turned out, it was just as well he hadn't set up a strong seduction scene for tonight, but then with Paula that would never have been a certain line. The distance which she seemed to insist on, however tender the moment, was a personal aloofness that she would have to deal with herself. He had confidence enough to wait and oblige her to take the final step towards him.

He had guarded against becoming vulnerable on her account, and he carried no photograph because she'd never specially given him one. He had only the group shots taken in their academic dress and posed on the steps of the Albert Memorial when Graduation had thrown them together. Just an alphabetic accident, because her 'Musto' followed his 'Mott' in the lists for Bachelors of Laws.

He went now to the folder where he kept the photographs and set them out along the mantelpiece. Paula, himself, and the Yeadingses—Mike, his Guv, and Mike's wife Nan. These two had been his guests at the ceremony, and Nan had since encouraged the Angus-Paula interest. Not that he lacked initiative himself, and for all her independence Paula had clearly shown a warmth that promised more. He looked now at her picture, at the calm brows, wings of dark hair, the serene smile that yet had a hint of mischief at one quirky end. Such a lovely face. You saw more in it to treasure every time you looked.

'Bloody *wet*,' he accused himself, impatiently swept the photos together and wedged them back in the bookcase, between his second-hand sixth edition of *Deep Diving* and the paperback *Bachelor's Book of Casseroles*. Briefly he wondered if the placing weren't haphazard but subconsciously significant. No, it was accident. Just as accident had landed him here tonight alone, empty and far from gruntled, while Paula was stranded at some unbooked West German hotel like so much luggage gone astray.

Early next morning he rang BA Inquiries as advised. Paula was listed on the first flight out, LH030, due in at nine-ten. The car was ready loaded with his luggage, and his passport in his jacket up to date in case they crewed across the Channel. Both he and Paula were virtual beginners at sailing but Barry was an experienced skipper and wouldn't hang around offshore. Angus gave him a ring with new instructions, to expect them mid-afternoon, and set off again for Heathrow.

This time the flight was dead on schedule and there were no delays at Immigration. The travellers flooded through into the main hall of Terminal Two wheeling trolleys, hugging and kissing at reunions, chattering in half a dozen tongues: but none of them was Paula. They thinned and there came a lull before the next arrivals. Angus buttonholed an airport official to go and dig Paula out of Customs. He came back to say that the whole place was clear and the next load just due.

She couldn't have changed so dramatically in a fortnight that Angus, posted at the exit gate, had let her walk right past. In any case she would have recognized his substantial bulk planted full-face at the crowd's front. She just hadn't come through. So where was she?

He showed his warrant card at the gate and, accompanied by a security man, was let through to Arrivals lounge. A new flight came in and all was activity again. He moved against the flow to where the heavy luggage was circulating on the carousel. In the scrimmage he thought he recognized one of her red cases. She'd had two, with chrome letters under the handle. Always two, medium-sized, because she found them easier to manage herself than one large one.

He plunged forward, muttered excuses and grabbed it. No chrome initials. The full address on a stick-on label was that of a Mrs P. R. Slater of Peterborough. He pushed the case back on its rounds and waited until all the luggage was cleared, but Paula's never appeared.

An hour later found him tight-lipped and apprehensive. Lufthansa had at last assured him that the lady definitely had not boarded the flight she was listed for, and her luggage remained unclaimed at Frankfurt Departures. There was no vacancy on any later flight. Indeed they had received no request from Miss Musto for an alternative seat. They could only conclude that the lady had suddenly decided to stay on in Frankfurt without informing airline or tour operators.

Angus had had enough. 'Book me there,' he told the Fiesta Tours rep shortly. 'You've got a phone, use it. It's your company that's lost her and this is an emergency. Say how much and I'll write a cheque now. Only get moving. I want the next plane out. There just has to be a cancellation.'

They passed him from official to official. All were scrupulously polite and increasingly uneasy. Somewhere along the line his persistence, or his argument, made its point. Patting his pocket to ensure he still had his passport, he abandoned holiday luggage and car, grabbed his overnight grip, phoned Chichester with a fresh message for Barry and boarded the BA flight due off at eleven-thirty. He caught it by the skin of his teeth, a security car taking him out to the Boeing by special delivery.

Three hours later he had the duty receptionist at the Hotel Bristol, Frankfurt, almost jumping through hoops for him. But to no avail. Miss Musto had checked out early that morning, having settled for her room service extras in Greek drachmas. All other costs had been met by the airline as part of their stopover service. As far as the hotel was concerned, they had no further responsibility.

CHAPTER 2

Frankfurt's Lufthansa office had been unable to help him about Paula's whereabouts. They too had checked that she left the Bristol without breakfasting with the rest of the delayed travellers from Greece. While Mott waited the desk clerk made phone calls to other hotels among which the Athens flight had been distributed and then collected this morning for their resumed return journeys. There were no reports of stray travellers in the public rooms and no new booking made in her name.

'One hope I still have,' the girl said eventually, laying down the phone. 'A thin one, do you say?'

'A slim chance.' He waited, frowning.

'Two persons at the Bristol have their journey broken. A Canadian lady wishes to visit her relatives in Köln while she is here. Another person, Palestinian male, is in hospital with injuries.'

'What kind of injuries?'

'Oh, that is a private matter, please.'

'I admire your discretion, but I am trying to find a missing person. I shall need to talk to him. There may be a chance he saw something relevant.'

'There were almost three hundred people on that OA flight,' she reminded him.

'How many stayed overnight at the Bristol?'

She looked at the list, ran a finger down the names.
'Fifteen.'

'So, let's have his name, also the Canadian lady's.'

Back at the Bristol they eyed him warily. News of his
quest had already spread among staff on the front desk.
They were being very correct, insisting on a phoned warning
to Mrs Drummond that her room number had been required
by an English gentleman in the foyer. Mott heard the
clear-toned answer from the receiver direct. 'Well, send him
up then.'

Room 402 was almost opposite the lift as he stepped out
of it. He knocked on the door. 'Mrs Drummond,' he said
when it opened, 'my name is Angus Mott. I've just arrived
from England and I need to ask you some questions about
a friend of mine.'

Mrs Drummond was tall for a woman, lean, erect, tanned
and apparently in her mid-sixties. She wore a well-cut silk
trouser suit in marbled strawberry pink and cream, and
white hair elaborately lacquered over an expensively pre-
served, good-natured face. The dark shadows round her
deepset, small brown eyes, together with sandals designed
for comfort rather than elegance, were probable pointers
that she'd clocked up a further decade that she wouldn't
advertise. She wore an impressive number of gold chains
round her neck, bulbous gold ear studs and an enormous
sapphire among her several rings. If the policeman in Angus
warned him that she was a sitting duck for a holiday gigolo
the thought died young when he encountered the shrewd,
confident gaze she turned on him. She treated him to a
splendid display of transatlantic dentistry. 'How can I help
you, young man?' she demanded directly. She wasn't in the
least astonished, a lady well used to being asked for aid.

'I believe you arrived here on Flight OA269 from Athens
and stayed overnight in this room, 402.'

'That is so. And I'm staying on another two nights until
it's convenient to join up with my sister-in-law in Cologne.

She lives there now. This stopover was a piece of luck for me.'

'I'm anxious to contact the young lady who used the adjoining room, 403, Mrs Drummond. I wonder if you can help me. I'm having some trouble getting in touch.'

She looked at him with her head a little on one side, doubtful whether she should point out that his interest might not be welcomed by the girl he was looking for. Then she suddenly made up her mind, smiled generously, stood back and waved him into the room. 'I'm afraid I can't help you very much. I assume she went on to England with the others. You must have just missed her.'

'What makes you think that? Did she speak to you at all, mention she would be leaving this morning?'

'No, I'm only guessing, because that's what everyone else did. She certainly had her overnight bag with her when she left. And she'd put her large luggage out in the corridor, as we were asked to do. It was real early. I only glimpsed her as I let the waiter in with my breakfast. I'd had it ordered for six-thirty on the dot before I decided to stay on.'

'Did she seem—quite ordinary in her behaviour?'

Mrs Drummond pulled a comic face, then chuckled. 'What's ordinary? Ordinary under the circumstances, I guess. She carefully avoided seeing me. Embarrassed, as she might well be.'

'Why embarrassed?'

'Oh, I don't want to spread stories.' Mrs Drummond waved well-formed fingers tipped with flawless ovals of strawberry pink enamel. The diamonds clustered round her sapphire threw a lot of light about. 'Not that she did come to any harm, but she was rather inviting trouble.'

A new flicker of alarm moved in Angus. 'How was that, Mrs Drummond?'

'Please don't Mrs Drummond me, I'm Kate. Can I call you Angus?'

'I'd be glad if you would.'

'Right, Angus, so why all this interest in my brief-stay neighbour?'

'I'd better declare myself.' He deliberately made it sound light, because he had the idea that any official approach would dampen Mrs Drummond's outgoing insouciance. 'Paula and I arranged to meet in London, there came this hang-up, so I met the plane she'd transferred to. Neither she nor her luggage arrived. I got a little anxious, so I flew out to check up.'

'Knight errant,' she exclaimed, fine-painted eyebrows nearly up to her immaculate hairline.

'Paula's the errant one. I'm left wondering.'

'Anxious,' Mrs Drummond corrected. 'Admit it, you think something bad's happened, don't you?'

'Maybe I'm over-reacting.'

She regarded him sombrely, head tilted. 'Mmm. I'd like to help, but there's little I noticed about her. Just the scene last night. It would be nine-fifteen or a little after. I'd come up from dinner about half an hour before to have a session with the telephone. Trying for this sister-in-law I mentioned.'

'You saw Paula?'

'I heard them. Voices coming from the elevator first, then outside in the corridor. They went into the next room, conversational at first; a little noisy laughter. Mebbe they'd had a drink or two over the top. They sounded young and having fun. And then it changed. She wasn't so amused. Alarmed and—and sort of shrill. Putting him off. Not how you'd expect it ending. He was insistent, getting real mad. He didn't raise his voice much. It was a dull rumble, but threatening somehow, talking fast. Then something got knocked over. There was a scuffle and some thumping. The girl squealed, not so much hurt as protesting, and I thought it had gone on long enough.

'I went and opened my door to the corridor, meaning to knock on 403 to shut them up. Not that I'm a fuddy-duddy over a little fun, but I just felt—a young girl mebbe out of her depth a little.'

'That was rather brave of you.'

'Foolhardy Kate, that's me. Anyway, I just had my hand up to knock on the door and it was flung open. The man came out breathing fire, smoke and alcohol, threatening all sorts of dire things in what I took for Greek. He was patting at one cheek with a folded handkerchief with blood on it. So I assumed that honour was vindicated and virtue unassailed, at any rate from the girl's viewpoint. She saw me watching though, hence the heavy embarrassment this morning.'

'And the man, did you see him again? Can you describe him?'

'No, I had just the one glimpse of him, with his face partly covered. But he was dark-skinned, with a lot of black curly hair, lean, probably under thirty, clean-shaven, my height —that's five ten. Say one-fifty pounds. Fleshy nose with a high bridge.'

Considering that her first word had been 'no', that was a good entry for the Description Stakes, Angus thought. He willed himself towards professional detachment to overcome the gut-churning the woman's description of the scene provoked. And this had been only one evening in Paula's fortnight of lone-girl holiday. If only he'd been able to get his own leave brought forward on the rota, and the tour operator's list hadn't been fully booked. If only, if only . . . 'How dark?' he pursued. 'A black?'

'Mediterranean. Like I said, he could have been Greek, an islander. But then he could have been a lot of things— Turk, Persian, Lebanese. I'm not too well up on these ethnic types. My kind of men were always pink and slightly puffy with a tendency to go thin on top. This one was real lover-boy stuff, but tough with it. Rather nasty under the skin was my impression, though I didn't encounter him at his best, as you'll appreciate.'

'So, apart from that encounter and then seeing her leave at about six-thirty a.m., you never saw Paula again?'

'That's right. But previously I had literally run into her on the plane yesterday. We both went to the starboard john about the same time. There were two in the tail on that side, and afterwards I followed her back towards our seats. A man on the gangway suddenly stood up to reach for something in the overhead locker and his elbow caught her so that she cannoned back on me. We were caught unawares because as we walked we were both looking down at the Alps through the starboard windows. It gave her a nasty shock and she was real mad at the poor dumb ox. Stood there white and shaking, with her wig slipped over one ear.'

'*Wig*, Mrs Drummond—er, Kate?'

'Wig, Angus. She had this long, Cleopatra hairstyle, but it wasn't her own. Oh, mebbe you didn't know that and I shouldn't have said.' She seemed more distressed at her fashion gaffe than at revealing Paula's entertaining a man in her room. This quirk put Angus off track and he let her hurry his departure without putting further questions to her.

'I hope you won't think it rude of me,' she excused herself, clinking the room key against its tag suggestively, 'but I promised myself a quick shopping tour of Frankfurt before I join my brother's ex-wife. And time's slipping away, nice though it's been meeting you, Angus.'

He thanked her and moved towards the door, allowing himself to be manipulated.

'Look,' she said impulsively, 'I'll give you my sister-in-law's telephone number, just in case you need to get in touch again. I'd like to be sure you catch up with your girlfriend.' She scribbled on a piece of paper taken from her handbag and offered it.

'Thanks, Kate,' he said and let her dismiss him.

His next visit was to the injured man in Frankfurt's main hospital. He found him sitting out in the day room, his face

decorated with strips of adhesive dressing and his left wrist
high in a sling on the opposite shoulder. Broken collarbone,
Angus assumed.

With his Anglo-Saxon fair skin there was no hope of
passing himself off as a relative of the patient when the
Ward Sister bore down on him and the obliging student
nurse who'd made the identification. Angus was reduced to
showing his Thames Valley warrant card, although it could
have no pull without the local force's authority. It worked
in this case, however, and by the Sister's down-turned mouth
he guessed that she had little sympathy for the man who
had excited police interest.

His name showed him to be an Arab, and he spoke
no German. When Angus addressed him in English he
brightened and said, 'Hey, feller, get me some orange juice,
will yuh? They pretend they don't understand me.'

The man in the next chair was asleep and no one seemed
to be watching. Angus went round to a table on the sleeper's
far side and unscrewed the cap of a squash bottle. He poured
some into a tumbler and added water from a carafe.
While the dark-skinned man drank it off Angus leaned
against the wall. 'What happened?' he opened conversa-
tionally.

The Arab had got into a fight, didn't remember the details
because he'd had a load on. Had a date with a chick which
went flat. Dames didn't stand him up, no way, and he'd
gone out on the town, taken on first some more schnapps
and second a surly local who just happened (they told him
later) to be a river-boat's cook and the whole crew were in
the tavern with him. So there was a barney and he woke
up here. And was supposed to be in London. A bad way to
start a job abroad.

His American-English was good, if heavily accented. He'd
clearly picked up his colloquialisms from a genu-wine NY
source. Given the spread of American TV programmes the
nurses certainly should have been able to understand him.

If they claimed not to, it confirmed their failure to find him respectable.

'You joined the plane at Athens?' Angus probed, taking him back to yesterday.

'Yeah, started in Rhodes, though. Changed at Athens.'

'Travelling alone?'

'Sort of. Picked a little chick up at Athens airport, going back to London. Seemed sort of lost, so I collected her boarding card with mine and we got seats together. Thought she'd be good for a tumble when we suddenly got this overnight stop, but I'd read her all wrong, it seems.' He grimaced ruefully and patted a dressing on one cheek.

Something prickled along Mott's spine. He looked hard at the other. Dark-skinned, lean, under thirty, lots of curly black hair, clean-shaven for the most part, fleshy nose with a high bridge. No coincidence surely. This could be Kate Drummond's ethnic type she couldn't exactly place. Small wonder, because he'd been internationalized along the way, a long way from the Prophet's ban on alcohol for instance.

'Nice place, the Bristol,' Angus suggested casually, standing straight as if about to leave.

The man squinted up at him through the dressings. 'It's okay. That where I met you? Don't remember,' he grinned.

'Think I saw you with the chick. Pretty girl, long dark hair on her shoulders. Good legs.'

'You got the hair right. I've sure seen better legs.' He shifted painfully in the chair. 'I could tell you about legs. Some chicks I—'

'No time to reminisce,' Angus said tightly. 'I have to go now.' Abruptly he made for the door before he gave way to the anger boiling up inside. He couldn't trust himself to go any farther with this animal. It was up to the local police. He had enough now to get them officially interested. All he needed was to check back with Heathrow that Paula hadn't meanwhile put in an appearance, and then she'd be entered as a Missing Person. And when the Frankfurt CID got round to questioning this turd in the hospital he wanted to be of their number. So, to make sure, he'd book a call person-to-person to his own Guv, Detective-Superintendent Mike Yeadings. Get a reference, lay on some official standing.

Yeadings was not available. The best Angus could do then was to phone the Guv's home number and pour out his sorry tale to Nan. Thank God she was a deal more clued than a lot of jacks' wives, and had a warm interest in his progress with Paula. She didn't offer any easy balm, just promised she'd get through to Mike somehow and let him know. She would also pick up his spare keys and bring the car back from Heathrow. No need to incur all that expense, and he could always return by taxi. Meanwhile, was there anything else she could do? How about Paula's luggage?

'It's being held here,' Angus told her. 'They wouldn't load it unaccompanied. And there's no question of my being allowed near it. Could Mike pull strings, do you think, and demand it's sent, freight, to await addressee at Heathrow? Then someone could have it searched. See if there's anything significant.'

'Better still,' Nan said quickly. 'We have a personal friend in Airport Security. I'm sure he'd open it and list the contents for you. If there's anything strange turns up, or fails to, Mike will put the bulldogs on it. Where can we contact you and when?'

'On present form I could be sleeping rough tonight, but I'll get the Bristol to take messages. Here's the number.'

'Fine,' she said, making a note. 'What's the time with you in Frankfurt? Seven-twenty, right. I'll try to have something for you in three hours.'

'Nan, you're wonderful!'

'Aren't we all? Keep at it, Angus. Somewhere Paula's waiting for you to catch up. I just know it.'

CHAPTER 3

He met a blank wall with the Frankfurt police department. They took notes on what he had to tell them of his interviews with both the Canadian woman and Riaz Hussain, but their disapproval increased as the details accumulated. His professional standing counted for nothing since he was personally involved. With mild curiosity they passed round his warrant card—a piece of local colour from a distant planet —and then handed it back without comment. Or effect.

An officer would be sent to question the injured man at the hospital, but it was out of the question to allow an outsider to sit in on the interview, the more so since he had a declared interest. He could, if he so wished, make an appointment to return next morning, about noon, by which time some information might be forthcoming. They could promise nothing, of course.

It was humiliating. Behind their correctness there was a barely concealed pity, varying from sympathy to macho scorn. He was in their eyes a rejected lover, a man who let his woman travel abroad on her own and deserved any outcome. When they came face to face with Hussain—a lover-boy but tough with it, as Mrs Drummond had said— what sort of girl would they imagine Paula to be? He had to admit it was out of character for her to encourage such a man's company for a matter of nine hours or more, let him pick up her boarding card and manage her luggage. The Paula he himself knew was too independent, too careful. So cautious in fact that he had seen fit to hold back when he might otherwise have swept her off her feet, thinking they'd all the time in the world before them and the relationship was too important to risk rushing his fences.

So he'd been wrong. On holiday her defences were

lowered to the level of Hussain's crude company, even if she'd chickened out of the final scene he'd had her set up for. Girls were such fools, but he'd thought Paula had more sense.

Well, you learned. And, despite it, he still felt the same way about her. Only maybe he'd treat her a little differently once he'd caught up again.

Of course, Hussain was a boaster. To another man he'd want to project the image of an experienced womanizer. So had his story been factually correct, or was it wishful thinking? He and Paula made an unlikely pair. Had he perhaps just seen her alone and aloof, from a distance, created the fantasy of her company on the plane and then later seized his chance at the Bristol to get her talking over a drink? It seemed a lot more likely because Angus didn't know how truthful Hussain normally was, and he thought he had known Paula. The obvious thing to do was to check out the theory on Hussain himself.

The hospital had by now changed over to night routine, lights blazing from the upper windows, its ground-floor rooms curtained. Through the glass doors the main reception area looked formidably empty and sterile. He'd get no welcome at this hour from the porters. At Casualty Entrance, however, there was bustling activity as two ambulances unloaded blanketed stretchers. Nurses and white-coated medics hurried about with trolleys, saline drips, blood bags.

Angus used the approach that had never failed him in gaining unhindered access to an English hospital. Look as if you're urgently needed and bloody late, was the advice he always offered his DCs if they showed alarm before gorgons in starched uniforms. He adopted the formula now, leaning foward for speed, jingling a ring of keys in one hand, tensely frowning ahead.

He found the right stairway, took the lift up to Hussain's floor. Night Sister was checking notes in the main ward under a spotlight; elsewhere it was dim. Angus stood in the corridor waving behind the woman's back until one of the patients noticed him and correctly interpreted his pointings. Eventually Riaz Hussain, in a dressing-gown, came swaggering out expecting his new friend had brought him in a drink. They eased themselves into the lavatory unseen, and Angus came straight to the point.

'I bet you five pounds sterling,' he said, 'you can't remember a conversation verbatim.'

He had read his man right. 'Done,' Hussain agreed. 'What's "vergating"?'

'It means "in the original words". Still on?'

'On, sure. What conversation? The things we said when you came in early on?'

'No, let's try yesterday. You tell me what you and the chick on the plane said yesterday.'

'You want to know how I chatted her up? Hey, what is this, mister? You *audio-voyeur* or something?'

'Nothing like that. But it just happens I know her too. It's a way I thought of to check on something she said. You can't always believe what a girl tells you.'

Hussain continued to look slyly at him under his eyelashes. 'Okay, then,' he said at length. 'For five pounds, eh?'

Angus extracted a note and held it between his fingers suggestively.

'She said "Sorry" in English when she stepped back on my toe. I got a look at her label on the hand luggage. Her name looked kinda Italian to me.'

'Paula Musto,' Angus said slowly. 'Musto is an English name, though.'

'Hey, you *do* know her then! I thought you were kidding. Look, I never laid a hand on your girl, man. She never gave me a chance . . .'

'Take it easy. All I want is the conversation, as I said. Where was it you met up?'

'Athens airport. I already told you, I offered to see her big luggage on the belt, and then I grabbed a couple of seat numbers for us from the tour guide feller. We were both booked with Fiesta, had the same luggage labels.'

'Where did you sit?'

'Pretty near the back. Six, seven, rows up. This side the plane, looking forward.' He held out his good hand.

Starboard, as Mrs Drummond had said. And the man hadn't hesitated.

'So, the conversation.'

Riaz Hussain launched on his chatting-up routine and Paula's responses. They grew increasingly unlikely as the man went on. Angus felt a hot flood of anger rising inside him. Hussain was lying glibly, happily earning his fiver with a total fabrication.

'Well, we had this bottle of *retsina* to finish off and she was good 'n' happy on it so I lit some grass and passed it to her. I thought she was teasing when she said she hadn't smoked a joint before. She was only carrying *Gauloises*.'

Angus had almost given up listening. He was too hard at it convincing himself that he mustn't knock the daylight out of a man with a broken collarbone. But then Hussain's tone of complaint came through and it rang with genuine chagrin. 'I guess now she wasn't foolin'. I took her for a real hot-pants, y'know, man. But she was no more'n a prick-tease. Turned me right off when it came to the joy bit. I shoulda made her just the same. Maybe she wanted it rough. Not that she woulda been any good. Too thin. I never thought mucha going to bed with a bicycle.' Carried away by the memory, he had clearly forgotten the connection between Paula and the man questioning him.

Angus held out his hand with the fiver in it and let it drop into the other's clutch.

'Hey, if you're coming back . . .' Hussain began.

Angus shook his head, still walking out. Where now, he wondered, as the heat began to leave him, fiercely striding along the embankment. He could do worse than return to the Bristol and wait for Yeadings or Nan to contact him. He supposed he should eat too. He'd had nothing since lunch on the plane, but he wasn't hungry. There was a deep dull ache low down in him, but it was more akin to rancour than to emptiness. Anger at having been so fooled by a lovely face and his own need for a kindred spirit, because at last Hussain had convinced him. He'd exaggerated the conversation but he hadn't made up the entire Paula episode, because such a boaster wouldn't manufacture a story where he was the one rebuffed. The man was too fond of himself for that. But the Paula of Hussain's pick-up wasn't the Paula Angus was so hooked on. Over these last two weeks she was disturbingly changed. Not the same girl at all.

Mott halted in mid-stride. *Not the same girl at all!* Was that really the answer? Which was the simpler explanation to the seeming contradiction—that Paula, his Paula, affected by some sinister influence, should have undergone a change of personality, or that someone else had taken her place?

He didn't know which solution he cared for less, because if the latter, what had become of Paula herself?

The first person he ran into in the Bristol foyer was one of the plainclothes men from Frankfurt police bureau. He was turning away from Reception with a crumpled piece of paper in his hand. 'Ah, Mr Mott,' he said in evident embarrassment. Both men gave Angus the now familiar look of awkward sympathy.

'Your telegram, sir. I'm sorry,' the receptionist murmured.

Light broke on Angus. 'The one I sent Miss Musto from Heathrow? Didn't she get it?'

'Oh, indeed, sir, yes. Although it was phoned in, the duty clerk could not get an answer from her room. So it was transcribed and put under the door next morning, early.'

He was clearly trying to cover up a suspected bungle and it
made him nervous. 'It is the normal procedure we . . .' He
moved his hands expressively.

'So?'

'What he means,' said the German detective heavily, 'is
that your lady see the telegram, then she put on her clothes
quick and leave the hotel.'

'Yes,' Angus said thoughtfully, 'I see.' He wasn't bothered
by the pitying glances both men turned on him. 'Would you
ring Room 402,' he demanded, 'just in case Mrs Drummond
has retired? I want to see her again.'

'As you wish, sir,' the receptionist granted reluctantly.
He spoke into the receiver and handed it across.

'Angus!' Mrs Drummond said delightedly when he announced himself. 'Have you found your Paula already?'

'I'm afraid not, Kate. Still asking questions. Could I come
up if it's not too late?'

'Well, of course. I have a very smart wrapper I'll put on
specially.'

Angus handed the phone back. 'There should be a call
for me from England in the next half-hour. If I haven't come
down will you have it put through to Room 402?'

'As you wish, sir,' the man said again, scribbling a note
on his pad.

'And if I need to get in touch with the officer dealing with
this case,' Angus asked the detective, 'what name shall I
ask for?'

The man looked bleakly back at him. 'Herr Niedhart. I
write for you his extension number.' Angus pocketed the
piece of paper and strode purposefully back towards the
lifts.

Upstairs Mrs Drummond was waiting for him with the
door ajar. Her air of seriousness belied the coy phone
manner. 'You must be really done in. And I guess you've
not eaten?'

'Later maybe.'

'Later nothing. I'm *stumm* until you've at least a chicken sandwich inside you. Just wait while I phone down. White bread or rye?'

She gave specific orders to whoever answered her buzz, then she lit a kingsize cigarette, offering Angus one which he refused. 'Shoot then. I'm ready for the questioning.'

He watched her sitting opposite, the pale smoke coiling thinly upwards from the elderly, manicured hand. 'Did you smoke on the plane?' he asked slowly.

'I always do. Not that I'm nervous exactly, but it helps me not to be.'

'So you sat towards the rear. On the starboard side, you said.'

'About ten rows forward of the john, yes.'

'It seems that Paula smoked yesterday, so she would have been in the rear part too.' He was still calling her Paula because he wasn't completely sure even yet. But his Paula refused even mild cigarettes, certainly wouldn't have carried *Gauloises*.

'Then she was probably behind me somewhere. I never saw her seated. Just in the gangway when we collided.'

'And her wig was knocked sideways. Have you ever worn a wig, Kate?'

'Have I *not*?—dreadful things! Always make my skin *creep* after half an hour. Never wear one unless my hair's a real bird's nest and I have a special occasion to dress up for. Just for vanity, I guess.'

'Could that be why she wore one, do you think? But wouldn't it be uncomfortable on a four-and-a-half-hour plane journey?'

'It surely would be for me. But I'd say she wore it for the colour. She made quite a pretty brunette. Maybe she'd had black hair for her passport photograph and changed it in between.'

'You mean you saw the colour underneath and it was different?'

'Why yes, didn't I say? Her own was nothing special, sort of light wispy stuff as far as I could see.'

There was a silence. 'Angus, have I said something wrong? Is there anything else the matter?'

'Just a nasty suspicion, but I have to make sure. Kate, will you describe Paula to me, in detail like you did that man you saw her with?'

'I'll try. She was not so tall, say about five feet four. Fine-boned, narrow shoulders and hips. Kind of skinny, but quite heavy in the legs.'

Mott closed his eyes, remembering Hussain's comment. 'And her face?' He conjured up a vision of Paula's perfect oval, the dark winging brows and wide smile.

Kate was frowning in concentration. 'Pinched. Skin a little on the dry side. Maybe she was short-sighted. Pale eyes, quite large: her best feature. Her nose went up a bit at the end and it lifted her upper lip, showed two prominent teeth. D'you know what I thought?—Minnie Mouse!'

'Thank you.' Mott swallowed harshly. 'That's a marvellous description, Mrs Drummond. You're unusually observant.'

'Kate,' she corrected him. 'That slip you just made there means I've upset you. I didn't want to.'

'A marvellous description,' he repeated. 'But it wasn't Paula's. Whoever came through from Athens yesterday with Paula's hand luggage and passport and tickets was a complete stranger.'

He stayed on in Room 402 to ring Herr Niedhart's number and dictate a note on his new discovery. The phone call from the Guv came through straight afterwards.

He listened while Angus brought him up to date. 'So I'm leaving it with the local force to find who it was took her place, and I'm going on to Greece, because Paula never left it. She's been lost at least thirty-six hours now. Maybe in Athens I'll find someone who actually saw her.'

CHAPTER 4

Today was Friday, Angus had to remind himself firmly. So much disjointed travel and frustrated communication played the devil with your sense of time. Forty-one hours now since Paula had been due to touch down at Heathrow. Two whole days since she had failed to board the plane. A lot could happen in that time. Every hour wasted meant her tracks more covered over, the past less retrievable. It was like sitting in a boat's stern to watch the wake's V spreading, flatten, disappear, become just so much unidentifiable water in a sea of the same. *Wake*, he thought. Oh God, that was a terrible word to come to his mind.

He was waiting. Again in a police office, but this time in Athens, and it was an ironic branch of Hell for a man to be confronted so by his own kind. He knew too well what the flat eyes, the throwaway remarks, the limp movement of papers over a desktop meant. They were familiar gestures from his own repertoire. Here there was no welcome for him as a colleague, but the same closing of ranks against him that he'd met with in Frankfurt. Because he was on the wrong side of the desk: one of Them instead of Us.

But here there was a difference. In Frankfurt's stone-walling there had been a hint of national rivalry. In Athens something more. They were distinctly wary, *expecting* trouble more than immediately refuting it. He supposed they had a reason for this: too many newspaper headlines about detainees jumping from headquarters windows, too many dogged attempts by foreigners to dig up closed files on murdered relatives, rake over old outrages. Well, the Greeks weren't uniquely vulnerable: all over the free world police premises were being selected as the ideal springboard to launch political scandals. At home it wasn't only the militant pickets who threatened law and order. In his own Force they experienced a similar attack, if slightly milder, from Leftists on their Police Committee.

So, for the present he was on the wrong side, one of Them, and passivity was the only acceptable pattern. He had to submit, had to sit and answer police questions, had even to wait until an official found it convenient to come and ask some. And all the while more water streaming out behind the boat, becoming unidentifiable in the mass of the sea. Paula getting further lost as a police statistic.

He rose abruptly from his chair and went to lean his forehead against the window-pane, gripping the sill in impotent anger. He was conscious of slight movement behind him, the note-taking uniformed man recrossing his legs under the table.

The window's glass, he noticed, was reinforced with wire net. And didn't open. This was not a room people jumped from. Perhaps, he thought bitterly, they keep a special one for that.

The door opened behind him and two men in civilian dress came in, both new to him. The first, he saw at once, was Greek Security—fiftyish, of medium height, fit, compact. His bland, round face, like a browning grapefruit, had its features set reticently back. The man's eyes were as dark and cold as basalt. He nodded unemotionally, once in greeting, again to indicate the table. As Mott moved back towards it the second man came eagerly forward, full of professional bonhomie, and stuck out a hand. 'Justin Barlow,' he introduced himself, beaming, 'from Fiesta.'

Mott touched his fingers briefly and looked questioningly over his head at the other. The brown grapefruit allowed the hint of a bleak smile to escape him. 'The travel company Miss Musto was touring with,' he said in perfect English. He made no attempt to introduce himself.

'Well, that's something,' Mott granted. He faced the smaller man, an excitable dancing-faun type with thick lenses to his spectacles and a waggish little beard. 'What can you tell me?'

'Please be seated, Mr Mott,' the Security man said smoothly. 'I appreciate the pressures on you, but bear with us a moment. I understand from Mr Barlow that he did not personally meet Miss Musto when she changed planes at the airport, apart from momentarily when issuing the boarding cards.'

'He didn't then,' Mott said bluntly, 'because it was a different girl in her place, and she had a man pick up her seat ticket with his own.'

Justin Barlow was only briefly off balance. 'You understand, there wasn't a great deal of time to spare. I'd two groups to combine for Flight 269, one from Rhodes and the other from Crete. Not a single face I remember seeing from earlier. They were just a list of names to me. Well, you know how it is. No, how can you? It's Babel and Bedlam both together. A forest of waving arms. They'd trample me down and snatch the whole bunch of cards if I didn't get a porter's trolley between me and them. Talk of lions at feeding time!'

'But you have an identifying system?'

'Of course there's a system. The bloody clever computer sets it up, doesn't it?' The little man was really rattled. 'And we all know computers can't make mistakes. But the durned machine doesn't have to stand out there and face the lunatic mob. Everybody's tired, and they haven't tasted a proper pot of British tea for a fortnight, and their sunburn's giving them hell, and the wife's gone off to the loo for six weeks and little Jimmy's just bust the Greek vase they bought for the boss's secretary. Some chance a system has! I holler out the names, and one hand makes a wilder grab than the rest. Someone shouts a number and I peel off so many cards in a bunch. They may be whole families. They may be lifelong buddies, or they can just as well be fresh pick-ups, but I don't inquire. All I have is a wodge of neat printouts and a bloody battlefield rabid with a form of frustrated lemming-mania, and a set time to get them on the aircraft by. Anyone who wants my job can have it right now.'

'You see?' the brown grapefruit face demanded gently. 'It doesn't help much. But I thought you should meet him.'

'You didn't notice her either on the way here, a fortnight earlier?' Angus pursued hopelessly.

'On arrival, much the same. Just a sea of faces, not quite so wild though.'

'Not yet exposed to our Balkan excitability,' suggested the other man blandly.

'But she had a special booking,' Angus remembered. 'She wasn't continuing by air like the others. She was to stay here in Athens with a friend for the first week. Wouldn't she have asked you about a taxi or something?'

Justin Barlow looked suddenly smitten by painful recall. '*That* one? Oh my, oh goodness! I am sorry. Fancy anything happening to her!'

'Tell us,' the Security officer commanded.

'As you say, not one of the group to fly onwards. She was to stay her week in Athens with friends, then join the following week's influx from England, spend a single week in Crete, then return with the original group she'd left Heathrow with. It meant a little more organizing because I'd a free seat to off-load on the first Athens-Iraklion flight and an extra one to obtain on the same flight a week later. You follow?'

'Never mind the office details,' Mott glowered. 'You remember the girl, what she looked like?'

'She was a honey. Cool, amusing, really interesting to talk to. I don't often get the chance . . .'

'So you spoke with her when she arrived?'

'More than that. Once I'd cleared the mob through to Departures I gave her a lift to where she was staying, out at Voula.' He blinked earnestly. 'That's on the way to Sounion, you know,' he added, remembering his tour guide responsibilities.

'Voula's where she stayed on the mainland,' Angus agreed. 'I had a card from her there. Later I had cards from her posted in Crete. Did you see her when she joined the later group to go there?'

'I did. Just a glimpse. She waved but we didn't get a chance to talk. She looked fine. The new suntan suited her.'

'Can we assume that she actually left on that plane for Iraklion?' the anonymous man asked silkily.

'Oh yes, definitely. I—er—watched her go on board. No one came off after that. She left here all right. She certainly got as far as Iraklion.' His relief was evident. He sat back now from the edge of his chair and wiped an immaculate handkerchief over the ridge his spectacles had left on his nose.

'So you will continue yourself, Mr Mott, to Iraklion?' asked the bland-faced man with the cold, dark eyes.

Mott nodded. 'As soon as I can get a place on a plane.'

'That is already arranged.'

Angus looked hard at him, conscious once more of being manipulated. But Iraklion was where he certainly must be to pick up Paula's traces. The island of Crete was where her cards had come from and there was no doubt in his mind that Paula had written them herself. She had a distinctive hand and there were private allusions no one else would have known about.

'We have time for lunch first,' the Security man announced urbanely, dismissing the Fiesta courier with a cool nod. 'And then I shall give myself the pleasure of driving you back to the airport. You can tell me meanwhile how my old friend Mike Yeadings has settled down in Thames Valley. I first met him at an international Police Conference and later was on loan to London when he was with the Met. My name is Mikhailis too. Mikhailis Kostantinou, at your service.' He bowed from the waist. Without a flicker of expression the secret policeman had become a social charmer.

They were met with a lot of smart saluting on their way out of the police HQ and it was clear to Angus that this man was one of their Big Fish. And a friend of the Guv, which made a difference. Angus should have known Mike Yeadings wouldn't let grass grow under his size eleven shoes. He must have phoned through to his old Greek acquaintance immediately after speaking to Angus in Frankfurt.

At Athens airport there was further proof of his quick reactions. He'd arranged for some enlarging and copying of the Graduation photographs, a set of which he and Nan had kept as a memento. Then photocopies had been made of pages from Paula's holiday diary found in her main luggage on its delayed arrival at Heathrow. Mike had enclosed a separate set of all these for Angus inside the package addressed to Mikhailis Kostantinou. It was waiting for them at the airport where the Security chief had obviously been advised to pick it up. The speed of the operation astounded Angus.

The Greek officer's calm assurance and the name-dropping in his reminiscences of London's Met, while they ate and drank at Glyfada Marina, had worked on the young Detective-Inspector's fatigue to dull his critical faculties. When Kostantinou made a detour out to Voula and pointed out Dímitra's villa where Paula had spent her first week in Greece, he fell in with the man's suggestion that such powerful friends should not be alerted to the girl's disappearance. They were outside the circumstances of it and any moves they made would be spectacularly publicized, endangering the necessary secrecy of police investigations. There could be risk to the missing girl if attention was turned on her connection with the Antoniades millions.

It was only when he was airborne that the first doubts struck Angus. He opened his own packet of photocopies sent through by the Guv and turned to her most recent diary entries. This confirmed his uneasy suspicion. There was nothing to prove that Paula had ever set out that last morning for Athens on the first leg homewards, because the diary must have been already packed. It was blank after the previous day's entry of *Goodbye drinks at K's,* which seemed the reminder for an engagement. But equally there was no evidence that she hadn't reached Athens as planned, and gone missing there. He had been fobbed off with the implication that his search must resume in Crete, leaving it to Kostantinou to check among the acquaintances Paula had made earlier in the capital and who might well have arranged to meet her when she changed planes on the return journey. So much depended, he saw now, on who and what the girl was who'd taken Paula's place. She must have gone missing *from* somewhere. Who was covering for her? Did Kostantinou suspect that she'd come from Athens? And were the Frankfurt police going to take up seriously the tracing of where she had gone after the Bristol? It seemed that the true hunt must be made from those two cities. And he was sidetracked to where the trail had already gone cold.

Desperately he took up the diary pages again and stared at the final entry. *Goodbye drinks at K's*—no time given, no place. From what he'd seen on the fascias above Athens shops, half of all Greek names began with a K. Mike's friend Kostantinou himself, for example.

The engines of the Airbus lulled him into half-sleep but he started awake with a sudden memory. Back in Frankfurt, another K. Kate Drummond who had seemed so sympathetic. Hadn't she come from Crete too? Or Rhodes? But maybe he'd confused her with Hussain.

Whatever the truth of it, he was going in the opposite direction. Every turn of the engine bore him farther from the tracks already uncovered.

The cabin lights blinked on then with the request to fasten seat-belts. The plane started to dip and circle over Homer's wine-dark sea and a bluish, misty isle. They were coming in to land at Iraklion, on the north coast of Crete. Crete, which the Greeks called Kríti. *And that began with a K as well.*

CHAPTER 5

Nine days earlier it had been black night when Paula landed at Iraklion. Only by peering out so close to her port window that she shaded out her own reflection and the aircraft's bright interior did she first make out the darker island's coastline where a luminous creaming of waves broke along the shore.

The Airbus circled, dropping through a layer of fine mist, and suddenly there was a jazzy patterning of ground lights. Now the plane was over the city, falling swiftly towards brilliant orange-dotted lanes ahead. Sea and lights and buildings came sleeting up, the engine sounds changed, she glimpsed a black runway streaming in below, and then the wheels made gentle contact. She had arrived in Crete, Kríti: a childhood dream at last come true.

All the short journey across from the mainland she had been secretly smiling, hugging the long-held promise to herself. The best part of her travels, saved for the last. Crete had had a very special place in the imagination of a solitary small girl, as part of the heritage from her frustrated romantic of a father, straitjacketed by a small-town law practice while he longed to be treading in the steps of Sir Arthur Evans, digging out and handling ancient artefacts, reconstructing spectacular halls and galleries from visions of lost splendours.

He had made the journey himself only once, as an undergraduate of Merton, and ever after had had to content himself with dreams. But there was no pamphlet, news-sheet or coloured illustration of the digs that he hadn't collected and pored over later in his study back in Lewes. These were what served him whenever his little daughter begged for a bedtime story. The two had shared them with a special private glee, as though these pictures and stories were theirs alone, no one in their circle seeming equally to feel the lure of Knossos and Santorini.

The accumulated debris of æons and of vast earthquakes had had to be penetrated by imagination as fully as by the physical act of digging. Now she was to stand on the ancient sites themselves and the two would come together. In some undefined way it would also be a salute and farewell to her dead father, whose image had always vaguely overshadowed the living men who came her way. Recently she had admitted that she must free herself of his ghost, because she found she couldn't speak easily of him to Angus, and she needed him to understand her completely.

The fact of arrival seemed barely credible to her now, adult and stepping down the aluminium stairs to stand on Cretan soil. This was the culmination of her growing up, of surviving the alien world her restless mother had created after Father died. It was fitting that now, as she had completed her training, was ready to begin a career not so different from the one he had chafed under—but for her a chosen path, not second best—she should venture her scant savings in search of the double-tiered past that was at once her own and that of a vanished civilization.

Athens had been wonderful, of course, but not what she was targeted on. The week spent with Dímitra, one-time student friend in London and now transformed into a junior executive in her father's shipping empire, had lacked no luxury or delight. In Dímitra's cream Merc Sports they had visited Corinth, Mycenae, Epidavros. At Delphi she had scrambled along a rock passage to the Oracle's cramped cave. She had breathed the air in deeply, but no lingering scent of burning laurel or hallucinatory drugs remained. She had felt no vibes, and came out into the sunlight laughing.

Time, under this clear white brilliance, had different, deceptive values. Dímitra herself, so classically perfect in profile and now also so svelte, belonged to two periods, a modern who might yet have stepped down from a plinth of Praxiteles and taken on bright colour. And the city—mostly no more than forty years old, built up since the war's devastation—would suddenly be punctuated by crumbling pilasters and fallen pediments where two ages equably jostled. But mostly for her, despite the ever-visible Parthenon crowning the Acropolis, Athens was not old enough. Farther back in time, deeper in earth's strata, there was the Minoan Age of Crete.

Each breakfast-time at Dímitra's she had stretched her limited vocabulary to follow the local broadcast listing cars allowed for that day into the city. 'Registrations ending in zero to four,' she would shout up to the Greek girl still busy at her mirror. And Dímitra would groan comically and call back, 'Then today we must go in with Ioannis Doulapoulos in his Beetle and laugh at his unfunny jokes.'

At first it was a good idea of the government to halve the city traffic flow, save fuel and cut the carbon pollution which attacked the ancient monuments. But then, Dímitra explained, quite ordinary families began to buy a second car, so that there was always some transport for going to work. Whichever was the forbidden registration for the day was then used by the newly emancipated wife who doubled the carbon pollution with her bonus from the suburbs.

There were many Athenian stories about well-meant legislation which ironically defeated its own intentions. They were an ingenious people and took a lively delight in finding their own ways of extracting benefit from any changes introduced. It offered little hope that their inclusion would serve to iron out existing EEC anomalies.

Yes, she had wonderful memories of the mainland, of delightful people encountered, inspiring beauty of statuary and architecture, fascinating glimpses of family life in the crowded *Plaka* where she had lost herself on a visit to the Flea-Market; but it was Crete she had set her heart on many

years before, so this was a private pilgrimage she entered
on now.

As she claimed her luggage and saw it stowed into the
coach's hold, people passed between her and the velvet,
moonless night. Beyond the floodlights of the Arrivals hall
she could make out the shape of palms and something like
eucalyptus trees stirring in the breeze which islands always
seemed subject to. Taking her place inside the coach, she
reminded herself she was not encapsulated. There had to
be encounters outside her private requirements. She looked
for the woman she had sat next to in the Airbus from Athens,
but already she had found a seat and a receptive ear, pouring
herself out to what must be a lone male whose casual dress
and roving eye declared he was aware of his rare status and
only momentarily commandeered by the widowed ex-
schoolmistress from Runcorn. He met Paula's gaze now with
a bold challenge and she went farther down the gangway, not
to be seen as on her own.

Most of the other tourists were couples or in larger groups.
Half way down the coach was a vacant seat. Paula slid into
it with a smile at the elderly woman beside her. The one
she received back was meant to be gracious, but prim.
Permafrost beneath, Paula wondered, or had it been a mark
of self-defence?

Looking around, she supposed that after a few shared
meals and excursions these disparate persons would somehow become a unit and open up to each other. They would
have a brief week or two of close living, then part, never to
meet again. A few lasting friendships might result, perhaps
some animosity, but mostly the new acquaintances would
fade to mere conversational reference points once the travellers reached home laden with group photographs.

She resigned herself to the social niceties. 'I'm Paula
Musto,' she offered the prim woman. 'From London, a
student.'

'How do you do,' said the other, formally and not as a

question. 'My name is Pallett. Mildred Pallett, Miss. I come from Salisbury, Wiltshire, and I suppose you could say I was retired.' Her thin, over-refined voice took on an attempt at humour. 'Not that I've ever done much to retire from. I travel quite a lot, like this, but it's the first time I've come to Crete. I thought that this year I would have a change from the mainland. How about you?'

She can't expect me to compete in placename-dropping, Paula protested silently. I'm a third of her age and I've other uses for money.

Before she could prolong this patball conversation the tour guide's amplified voice demanded everyone's attention for a few immediate instructions before the *bouzouki* music took over again.

'. . . quite fond of gardening, although it does tend to strain my back,' Mildred was continuing unabashed. Paula closed her eyes and smiled, remembering her father who never could be a bore.

As the tour company rep moved down the coach Paula twisted in her seat and gazed after him. Quite different from the small, bright-eyed courier in Athens, this one was tall, already running to flab, with an unlined, ageless face, straight, floppy hair that fell between eyes and spectacles, a large nose (at present profusely sweating) and a loud Glaswegian voice. He had adopted a manner of exuberant confidence and determined youthfulness. He was theirs for the length of their stay and it was his job to be informative, helpful, entertaining. Clearly he took the name Fiesta quite literally. Popular he had elected to be, whether one liked it or not. There was little point, Paula saw, in resisting the self-cast fun show.

Already in the coach's rear there was an outbreak of bantering as he romped verbally with his new audience. Trivia of the journey, which might originally have grated, now were being served up in jokey packages; confidences were being exchanged between ladies, even before their names; men were grunting together in acceptance of each other's presence.

'I do hope,' said Mildred Pallett in a stricken stage-whisper, 'that this isn't going to be too *jolly* a party.'

She needn't have worried. As Andrew Whitelaw—'Call me Andy; everyone does—' came back to claim his microphone by the driver he stopped, bent low and asked earnestly, 'Everything as you like it, leddies?' He touched Miss Pallett's shoulder reassuringly. Was it all that hair in his eyes, or had he flashed Paula a wink, turning away?

'Just a little hulloo to you all on behalf of Fiesta and *mahsailf*,' he boomed through the amplifier. 'When we arrive at your hotel don't trouble aboot the luggage. Go straight through to the Maze Bar—aye, I did say *Bar*—where the management will welcome you with a glass of the local *ouzo*. Now mind, leddies, it may look transparent but there's a tiger in it all the same. You'll be needing to tak' plenty of water wi' it. While you're relaxing I'll come round with your room keys, timetables and so on. Also details of the complimentary coach tour of the city of Iraklion leaving the hotel tomorrow at nine-thirty. When you reach your rooms your luggage will already be there. No, no cause to worry aboot i'. There is no crime on Crete. We're all far too nice for tha'! As for your passports, I'll collect them as I go round the bar. Just ask for them back at Reception any time after eleven tomorrow morning. Now, have ye any questions?'

'I think he will manage adequately,' said Miss Pallett with new smugness. 'But I do wish he wouldn't shout quite so loudly.'

Circulating slowly among the party in the bar, Paula found that not all its members were as seasoned as Mildred Pallett. She had steered that lady to a cushioned bench where she delicately lifted an eggcup-sized glass of *ouzo* to her nostrils, declared she had never cared for aniseed, then downed it without a flicker of expression.

Paula was pleased to see that in different parts of the

room a choice of drinks was provided. She had become accustomed to *retsina* but she really preferred *raki*, the home-made firewater of mountain villages. Her choice made the purple-liveried waiter light up with joy. 'You like our *raki*? My father makes. I get you plenty, plenty!' he promised.

'Oh no,' she laughed. 'Never plenty! Just enough to fill a thimble. 'So!' She held up a finger and chopped off the top joint in mime.

The waiter rolled his eyes in mirth. 'Oh miss, miss,' he said and rushed off to find another connoisseur.

'You need to watch that stuff,' said the voice of experience. A boy of eleven or twelve leaned against a pillar and eyed her loftily.

'You sound as if you've learned the hard way,' she said, smiling. 'I didn't see you on the coach, did I?'

'Bet your sweet life you didn't,' Andy Whitelaw breathed in her ear, passing with an armful of papers and a bowl of keys with numbered tags. 'Des is a leftover from last week's arrivals, but in on all the free offers, you'll find.'

'By special arrangement,' the boy said in eyeball to eyeball challenge.

'As my guest?' Paula suggested.

'That's one way round it,' Andy conceded, shook his hair wildly back from his eyes and plunged on into the crowd.

'Aren't you drinking?' Paula asked.

The boy produced a half-tumbler of orange juice from behind his back and grimaced. 'Actually I'd like some nosh. Let's go and hang over the *kebabs*.'

But there was competition for her company. Bearing down from either side were two cavaliers. Simultaneously, 'Do you play bridge?' demanded the phoney ex-RAF moustache and watery blue eyes, and, 'Are you on your own too?' asked the solo male whom the Runcorn widow had marked down on the coach.

''Afraid not. Yes, I am,' said Paula sweetly, smiled and moved on to where a thin girl much of her own age hesitated on the edge of the gathering. 'Can I get you a drink?' she offered.

The girl smiled almost wildly, her fingers tugging at a gold chain round her throat. Her gaze moved distractedly over the crowded room. 'I can't see Malcolm. He came down first, and he knows I don't like being left alone. Oh thank God, here he is!'

Paula turned to the man who had appeared at her shoulder. They were of equal height and she met his strange silver eyes with a kind of shock. He waited while she found words to cover her confusion, and she felt a brief flash of anger because he had seemed to expect the effect his appearance made.

'Malcolm—this is Malcolm,' the girl said awkwardly, to fill the silence.

'We both know I'm Malcolm, darling. What a little silly you are. You should say the lady's name first.'

'We haven't yet introduced ourselves,' Paula said swiftly. 'I'm Paula Musto, from London.'

The man flicked a glance at her ringless fingers. 'Delighted to meet you, Miss Musto. Melissa and Malcolm Bowles, from Pinner. Almost your neighbours, you might say, though London's a wide address.'

He was fishing for background and it amused her to supply it, since it mattered so little. 'Bedsitland,' she claimed, turning again to the wife. 'I share a flat in Fulham with two other students.'

'That must be fun,' Melissa said abruptly. 'I was going to sit Oxbridge Entrance once, but Uncle James wouldn't let me.' There was a little catch in her voice and Paula stared sharply at her, suspecting she was being made a fool of.

'Well, it's just as well you didn't, isn't it?' Malcolm asked coaxingly, as if his wife were a small girl or mentally defective.

Melissa's smile came slowly and transformed her pinched

little face. 'No. I mean, yes. Because now I've got you.' She put a hand on Paula's arm confidingly. 'We're married, you see. I'm Mrs Malcolm Bowles now.'

'Married three days,' Malcolm teased, 'and already, just now, you thought you'd lost me!'

'Silly me,' Melissa said. 'You wouldn't be silly like that, Paula, would you?'

Paula didn't answer. She was frowning slightly, because there was something so serpentine, so *coiled*, about this smooth young-old man with the silver eyes, and it chilled her. He was watching his wife now, a faint smile on his lips, then he looked at Paula, waiting again, as if he expected to see how his patience and cleverness with silly Melissa impressed her.

'Isn't *ouzo* sheer poison,' she said suddenly, to account for her expression. 'Or haven't you tasted it yet?'

They hadn't, so they moved on towards where the drinks were dispensed. Paula did another round of the room, picked up a few more names and tried to memorize the faces which went with them. There was a New Zealand couple in their mid-forties, called Scott, with nubile twin daughters Gaynor and Michaela. Paula liked it that the girls hadn't been mirror-imaged with similar names, but the way they'd handled their own individuality was taking divergence rather far. Gaynor was crimped and pallid in hyacinth-blue chiffon; Michaela was punk, her cut-off black jeans stretched over pipe-cleaner legs, and her baize-green hair, cut in spiky chunks, was as angular as her stance. Despite the heat she was wearing a sort of chain-mail shirt and gold kid pixie boots.

Paula grinned at her. At least she was positive, and certainly she attracted more attention than her conventional twin. *Alternatively* conventional, Paula corrected herself, because Michaela too had certainly been following a recognizable trend.

The parents, Joan and Johnny, were ordinary and

pleasant, sensible enough not to appear put out by any odd appearances. They seemed to have linked up already with an elderly couple who'd spent most of their lives in Malaya. They were British and the man, addressed as Colonel Martin, introduced his little, wizened wife as 'Cynth'.

'Weel,' Andy Whitelaw challenged Paula as she reached the door finally to escape, 'have ye made up your mind to stay? Give us a whirl, hey? Or are you straight off home again?' Bonhomie had turned his whole face by now into a glowing disc of grease.

'I think we're all going to last out the course,' she assured him.

'Coach tour of the city tomorrow, don't forget. Nine-thirty. And Fiesta's noticeboard is on the ground floor, right beside the lifts. Everything you need to know will be posted there. Okay? And your room number is 437. Good night, leddy, and sleep tight.'

The hotel was one of the earliest postwar buildings and the fourth floor, she found, was at the top. The lift deposited her in a sort of arborium of tropical plants with corridors to either side and an ironwork spiral staircase leading to a solarium. A sign pointed up it, indicating Roof Pool.

Very convenient. She would go for a swim when she'd unpacked, write up her diary in bed, and then lights out. Tomorrow would be her first day on Crete. She meant it to be a full one.

CHAPTER 6

'Eleftherías Square,' Andy Whitelaw offered them gener-ously, waving the hand not occupied with his microphone. 'Elefthería means liberty, and this is where it all happens. In the evening there's the *volta*, a sort of formal walkabout, with boys and girls in their separate groups eyeing each other and showing off, and whole families dressed up with their little ones along, plus even the odd dog or cat. The tourists come along to stare, and the locals stare back at the tourists. And half the shops stay open all night, because of a daylong siesta.

'And don't forget, leddies, when ye're buying anything at all, ye must haggle. It's half the fun of the sale, and they'll be disappointed if you fail to do so, apart from thinking ye're a wee bit affected by the sun.'

'I shouldn't think many of the locals here are typical Cretans,' sniffed Mildred Pallett. 'They look disappointingly urban to me.'

'Everyone on Crete has a village he comes from,' Andy countered, his sharp ears alerted. 'They flock into Iraklion to sell produce or work in the hotels, and they need to make money because they have so many daughters all needing dowries of a small house and a grove of olive trees round it. Only then will a girl be worth a good man's spending the rest of his life supporting her. And although the locals do well out of the tourist trade, they discover that with so many hotels shooting up the price of the land has risen too. So they must work even harder to keep up with inflation.'

'How many daughters have you got, Andy?' called a wit from the coach's rear.

'Thirteen at the last count,' claimed the Scotsman imperturbably, 'so you see, ah'm not all that lucky mahsailf.'

'I knew he was talking baloney,' said Ben Kimber, the Yorkshire bachelor. 'That dowry line is real tourist fodder if ever I heard any.' Seated beside him, the widow from Runcorn was earnestly taking notes in a little red book as they toured the harbour, the Venetian fort, the city walls, 25th August Street and the Cathedral Square.

'I bet,' young Des said, nudging Paula (who had paired with him because she had already fallen to Mildred Pallett's lot for breakfast and didn't wish to be accepted as half of a permanent duo)—'I bet she actually knows what Panto-krator Gate *means*.'

The two women across the aisle from Paula were speaking French. She had noticed them last night at the bar reception and avoided them because although her French was fluent —due to those early years of Mother's widowhood in Men-ton—it would embarrass her, in a typically British way, to have the fact advertised. Now, however, the women were missing out on the guide's prattle and more than a little disappointed.

'Andy, please,' Paula called, raising a hand to catch his attention. 'Some of us are French-speaking. Can you say the odd word to them?'

'Oh, ah'm tairribly sorry,' he said. '*Je regrette infiniment. Pour moi, mesdames, c'est toujours un grand plaisir de vous accueillir* . . .' He was off again, doing his thing in French.

The elder of the two women leaned forward and nodded her thanks to Paula. She had a striking face, dark, lean, taut, with faded sandy hair and long, narrow eyes set a little aslant over sharp cheekbones.

The other one was not young enough to be her daughter, but about twenty-eight years old. A junior colleague, Paula guessed, and not a very worldly one, gauche and a trifle too eager to please. Secretaries? Teachers? More like nuns in mufti. The question teased her and she stayed alert for clues to their origin.

While the coach squeezed its way through the traffic of 25th August Street and Andy, now bilingual, expanded on the Saint's Day procession from the Church of St Titus—a treat reserved for a later batch of Fiesta clients—the women resumed their conversation. ' . . . *A l'hôpital de St Luc j'en ai vu de pareil,*' the older one was explaining. '*On ne dirait pas un vrai malade, vous savez . . .*'

'*Quand même . . .*'

Well, that explained it. They were nurses, and even on holiday there was no way of holding down a good Sister

Tutor. Paula watched them unobtrusively. What link had made these two come here together? Surely the younger hadn't the mental grasp or experience to make a satisfactory companion? If she had had verve or humour it might have been a credible relationship. Perhaps circumstances had moulded it, or the two were related in some way. By a special affection for each other? Paula didn't think it was that. They seemed to have a quite normal attitude to men, the older one assessing with amused tolerance, the younger responding with a gauche sort of cockiness to any gallantries. Even eager to be noticed, as if too accustomed to being passed over.

She was just ahead of them later in the Cretan Tourist Office where they collected street maps of Iraklion and lists of the tours available. Andy was relinquishing them to local guides for excursions outside the city and was now restricted to being their Visiting Guru-Comforter-Confidant on tap in the Maze Bar between eighteen and twenty hours each evening. In case of emergencies between times he had left his home telephone number posted on the Fiesta notice-board.

'Can we phone for a date with your thirteen aforementioned daughters?' inquired the phoney flying-ace moustache with heavy humour.

Andy grinned. 'Why not? You can even come over and help rinse the nappies through, if you're so minded!' Something unexpectedly steely in his voice warned them off his private life, but the grin never faltered.

Well, he had a right to privacy and his own brand of relaxation, Paula reflected. Pumping enthusiasm into inert travellers and damping down the inevitable squibs must take enough energy, without counting all the paperwork involved between booking and the physical production of all Fiesta promised in the brochure. *Friendship International's Europe (South) Travel Association* was the company's name in full. It had taken some verbal manipulation to arrive at sufficiently striking initials, and the cautious Paula, first reading through its literature, had accepted that the information could also have suffered certain twists. So far, however, she had no complaints. This group of holiday-makers *was* friendly and *was* international, as promised. The hotel was pleasing, her room more than adequate, and the temperature outdoors several degrees higher than the average claimed. Dímitra had wrinkled her nose and asked why Paula hadn't used a more famous travel company, and why had she wanted to get mixed up with a lot of foreigners as well as Cretans? But then Dímitra hadn't known why Paula wished to steer clear of contacts. They hadn't been close enough friends for Paula to explain about her dead father's obsession with Crete. Angus was the only person she was ever likely to tell, and then it would be after she had laid her father's ghost, which she admitted privately was her own minor obsession.

Andy had taken his leave of the party on that bluff note of non-invitation, and Paula turned to find the older nurse holding out her hand to be shaken. '*Mademoiselle*, I am Irène Petitjean, and I thank you . . .' she began in careful English, ending her sentence with a gesture towards the departing Andy.

'*Il parle trop vite, n'est-ce pas?*' She smiled back at the nurse. '*Moi, je m'appelle Paula.*'

'*Enchantée.*' The woman gave her a swift smile of appreciation and drew forward her companion. 'May I present Sylvie Audoin. We—travel together.'

They stood talking a few moments and then moved in a group towards the entrance to the Archæological Museum. It had a look of Fort Knox, with a formidable gate system and a lot of uniformed guards standing around. Properly so perhaps, because the exhibits were priceless and the main source of Crete's growing prosperity through tourism. For a moment Paula hung back, then went to obtain a ticket. She couldn't expect to have the place to herself in mid-

season, and it was vast enough to ensure she could wander
off apart without causing offence.

It was easy enough. There was so much of fascinating
appeal that everyone found an individual line to follow up.
Paula spent a long time hovering over the tiny carved seals,
and only when the crowd thinned towards lunch-time did
she go on to find the frescoes from Knossos Palace.

She was glad then to be alone, because she knew she
couldn't have spoken. There was an actual, physical lump
in her throat which made it impossible. All she could do
was gaze and gaze, just as she had done at Delphi before
the bronze Charioteer. But here the frescoes were as familiar
to her as the wallpapers of her childhood home. Familiar
but also exquisite: the vivacious trio of court ladies, the
charging bull, the Prince of the Lilies.

She came reluctantly away, promising herself to return.
Outside the sunshine dazzled, the city hummed with traffic.
Birds shrieked and squabbled in the trees of Eleftherías
Square, unknown birds like magpies sprinkled with sand.
The cafés all along the north-west side of the open space
stretched out to the roadway in extended terraces crowded
with bright tables and chairs, striped umbrellas and awn-
ings. White-jacketed waiters strutted between them balanc-
ing trays of coffee and glasses. I wish—Paula thought
suddenly—Angus was here. I wish we'd been able to make
the journey together.

She found she had threaded between the tables and was
the subject of rival claims from two waiters poised to rush
for her custom. One, with cerise lapels, belonged to the green
and white awning, the other to the blue trellis-with-vines on
her other side. Unthinkingly she had stopped between the
two and provoked a new phase in their entrepreneurial war.

More tables were occupied to the right, which perhaps
implied better service. Yet she still preferred her own company and so pulled out an emerald chair from a round white
table.

'You may regret it,' said a dry voice from a few yards farther on. 'In about seven minutes the sun will be full on you.'

The man was stretched out comfortably at length, ankles crossed, hands clasped behind his neck. To meet her eyes he had to tilt his head back and peer from under the linen hat he shaded his face with.

'I can stand the sun,' she told him. 'It's partly why I came.'

'The rest of your reason was Knossos,' he surmised. 'It's all right; not telepathy. I saw you coming from the museum. In another world.'

She was glad the waiter took her order then because she was angry at being so transparent. When she answered, her voice was cool. 'I've looked forward to coming for a long time,' she said. 'And it certainly was no disappointment.'

He didn't ask—as so many people did—if she was on her own. He seemed to accept it. He was a loner himself. She didn't know why he should have started to speak to her, but she was sure it wasn't usual for him. They went on eyeing each other evenly. She noticed the length of him, the lean-ness, the emaciated hollows at greyed temples and jawline, the way his shirt collar—buttoned, with a sober tie—seemed a size too large for him. The skin of his face, which he had covered against the sun but now exposed, was a yellowish brown, his eyes a light green and set in wrinkles when he smiled. But he wasn't really an outgoing person, wasn't as relaxed as his posture suggested. He seemed tensed inside. *Tortured*, she thought and then was astonished at the exagger-ated notion. 'Have you been here long? In Crete, I mean,' she couldn't help asking.

'Forever.' His weight moved in the chair, then suddenly he struck down at the arm with almost savage impatience. 'Oh, just less than a year, I believe.' An expression that she could not interpret passed fitfully over his face, then he seemed to relax again. His voice, when he went on, was droll. 'I'm almost a native. Though it takes much longer than that to be accepted.' He lifted his empty glass straight up in the air at arm's length, without turning his head, and almost immediately the waiter came and exchanged it for a full one. 'There are advantages in being foreign,' he explained drily. 'No one expects to understand you. You're forgiven much.'

He hadn't attempted to intrude on her, never offered a drink or asked a personal question. In fact he had broken off contact already and languidly pushed the linen hat farther across his upturned face. Abrupt, rude? Nevertheless Paula warmed to him. When she paid her waiter, which she went back to the service bar to do, she asked, 'The Englishman out there in the sun, do you know his name?'

'That is Mr Foden, miss. He is here a long time. Even in the winter.

'He must like Crete very much then.'

The man's dark eyes seemed to go opaque. He stared past her, expressionless. 'Perhaps, miss. I don't know.'

Rebuffed, Paula moved out across the Square, making for the post office to mail her cards home. She wasn't hungry enough for a hotel lunch and had no intention of joining the afternoon excursion to the Minoan Palace of Knossos. The front desk manager had told her where the local buses ran from and she would go only when the main party's coaches had returned. After her first visit she would give up being so stand-offish with the others, but for the moment they had no claim on her. The roof pool enticed her. While the marshalled tour took place she would stretch out on a towel and devote a couple of hours to developing her suntan and to a further delving in the guide books.

When eventually she left the hotel young Des materialized beside her and attached himself. 'Be your guide,' he offered. 'I know all the short cuts.'

'Ominous words. Actually I have a plan of the city, thanks.'

'There isn't a good one. They leave out all the little alleys. Where d'you want to go?'

She looked thoughtfully at him. 'The Lion Fountain.'

'Nothing simpler.' He jerked his head for her to follow him through the traffic, but she took her time catching up on the far side. 'Des, I hate to ask you this, but—'

'"—does your mother know where you are?" At least it took you longer than most to get round to saying it.'

'So, does she?'

'Sure. Any time you ask she'll say, "Around somewhere, I think."' He mimicked a vague distraction, waved his fingers elegantly. Then half ashamed, explained, 'When I'm away at boarding-school she doesn't know what I'm up to, see? So she gets used to not knowing. Come the holidays, we go off somewhere new and I take time off exploring.'

'Much the story of my young life,' Paula said briskly. 'Only I wasn't even a boarder in term-time.'

'Not brung up proper. Just drug around,' the boy said in a Mrs Grundy voice.

'Here, there, and everywhere,' Paula agreed. 'But girls are kept on a shorter lead.'

'Natcherly.' He leered in a good imitation of adult male superiority. Then helpfully, 'Going shopping? I can show you the best places.'

They had gone round behind the Tourist Office, crossed a road and now were in a narrow alley with a row of close-packed shops on either side crammed with tourist *kitsch*, fashion goods, cameras, wines, glassware, jewellery. Where it all suddenly ended in a thronging cross-street, Des pointed ahead. 'Lion Fountain,' he announced.

'Buy me a bag of mixed fruit, will you?' Paula asked, handing over two hundred-drachma notes. 'And have a Coke on the change.'

'Cola or cocaine?' he demanded.

'Don't be daft.'

Her brevity delighted him. He went off crowing. After a

quick glance at her wristwatch Paula moved back along the road to the bus stop for Knossos. Des hadn't caught up with her by the time she climbed on board and took a twenty-seven drachma ticket. The cheapest guided tour for visitors, by coach, was nine hundred. So even when she'd paid a hundred drachmas for entrance to the Palace it was only equal to a seventh of the official tour fee.

The bus was full of cheerful, dumpy people who stared brightly at her, the only foreigner of the trip. She was careful to thank the conductor in Greek and was answered, ''S a pleasure, miss.' It was for her too. She was glad that, knowing so many Greek students in London, she had picked up some useful phrases. At Knossos they showed her where to stand for the return bus and everyone waved as they rattled off, bound for farther inland.

There were only two coaches in the parking place and no queue for tickets. She knew from diagrams that the modern way in was from the West Court, but she hadn't been prepared for the tunnel of dazzling bougainvillæa that formed the approach. Then she was mounting a sort of artificial plateau and the whole labyrinthine exposure of the dig lay open to either side and dropping away by half-excavated terraces ahead. Close by, warm and gritty to the touch, were great storage jars of golden baked clay, Ali Baba-shaped and covered with Minoan decorations. Beyond their pits rose the Evans reconstructions of inverted cypress columns coated with plaster and painted dull red. They held up the ochre sections of gallery, roofing over the copies of the fragmented frescoes she had seen at the museum. The ground all around was of golden sandstone with intrusions of other rocks which once had some architectural function.

She walked, over stones that burned through her sandal soles, to the lowest point and looked back, picturing the original elevation of five or more storeys, gallery on gallery up the hill. There would have been gardens too, at all levels.

Those ancient Minoan friezes had been full of stylized flowers as well as multi-coloured peacocks, gryphons, dolphins.

She went by the way her guidebook listed, from the Central Court through the South Propylæum, and climbed to the upper floor by the Magazines and the Great Hall, then down again to the Throne Room. She waited while a guided group took photographs and drifted off, then she crossed the Central Court to enter the East Wing where the royal apartments were supposed to be.

It was all 'supposed', and many archæologists since Evans had scoffed at his imagination. Nevertheless, he had seen more than a humpy green hillside where a farmer had turned up a few crocks and seals with carvings on them. He'd bought the site outright from its Turkish owner and after years of labour had unearthed this incredible treasure. Whatever the truth of the Minotaur legend, there was an actual labyrinth of rooms in the palace. And for acres around, underlying the present-day farms and vineyards, must still lie the rest of the city of Knossos.

When she came through the Custom House out into the afternoon light she was still in a dream. A dream tinged with sadness, because the past *was* past, and she had to imagine the ghostly shadows in the theatre below her. Again she found herself wishing that Angus could be here and share it with her.

A little breeze was stirring the dust now and it blew hair into her eyes. When she had pushed it back she saw she wasn't alone. Like a little cross-legged leprechaun in shirt and shorts the colour of the sandstone, Des sat there waiting. 'What do you think?' he asked, a little anxiously.

She didn't know. 'I *wonder*,' she said simply. 'I wonder what kind of music they had, how the food tasted, what games they played, what they laughed about. I think they enjoyed life a lot.'

Des nodded seriously. 'They played on pipes. And I'm

sure there were harps and drums. Perhaps tambourines. Bronze trumpets, do you think?'

'Bronze trumpets would sound fine and brave. Can't you hear them echoing over the valley in the dusk, with torches blazing in sconces along the walls and great braziers in the courtyards? You could sit here and watch the mountains go blue and disappear into the night. And smell blossom.'

'Woodsmoke too, resinous.'

They sat together staring out over the countryside. At last Des stirred and opted for the present, starting to suck an orange from the bag of fruit. 'Of course it's all guess work. Imagination,' he said gruffly. Then, prosaically, 'I knew you were coming out here, so I saved enough change for the bus fare.'

She looked at him, suddenly suspicious. 'Des, did you pay to get in?'

He looked angelic. 'There are other ways. If you're small. I often come.'

'You're the limit.'

'Have an apricot.'

They finished the bag of fruit between them, Paula conscious by now of having missed lunch, and Des always capable of taking on a challenge. Then Paula stood up again. 'I've still the South House to see. Will you wait?'

He nodded, aware when he wasn't needed. 'You'll have it to yourself. That's a bit the guides miss out, usually.'

She went on down, her sandals making no sound on the stepped walk. As she turned in at the door there was a sudden startled movement in the dark interior, a gasp of dismay. Then a giggle.

Damn, thought Paula, I've disturbed a pair of lovers. But before he swept his straw hat up to his disconcerted face she had glimpsed and recognized the man. 'Excuse me,' she said, turning away, and heard the stiffness in her own voice. Perhaps he hadn't known who she was, standing with her back to the light. But in any case, could it possibly matter?

He was on his honeymoon. No one would take it amiss if he found the Minoan Palace irresistibly romantic. Why then had he seemed so upset, almost vindictive towards her? But then, he had seemed last night to be very concerned with his own image, this man with the curiously silver eyes. Bowles, she remembered his name now. Malcolm Bowles, and his wife was Melissa.

It was not until she was at the top of the West Court again that she happened to glance back and saw a slim figure slip out of the South House and with face averted move round to join a group of tourists returning to a coach.

Not Bowles, and not Melissa, but someone she had certainly seen recently.

'Des,' she said quietly, nodding across to the coach. 'Who's that getting in now? Someone we know, surely?'

'M'm,' he said, looking where she nodded. 'The Prince of the Lilies. Or that's what my mother calls him. He works at the hotel. Front desk manager, I think.'

CHAPTER 7

As they crossed diagonally towards their hotel Paula was struck by the powerful white light that filled the first-floor windows of the lounge. The sun had barely gone down, and other artificial lights on that summer evening showed tawny and feeble.

'What on earth—?' Des started to say, then suddenly stopped. 'I know! They've come back. The film people. Last week they were doing some sloppy love-story beside the roof pool. Not much of a crew. About eight, with one mingy camera on an electric trolley. But they ran the film through afterwards on video and they all discussed it. You know, it's actually *work*, not just fooling about and pulling faces.'

'You think that's what all this light is for? The lounge

certainly wasn't like that last night. Rather dim and sleazy,
I thought, when I looked in.'

'So this is what they were haggling over on Friday with
the Manager,' Des declared. 'They must have hired the
room for some indoor shooting. Let's go up and see. Come
on!'

'Hi, you can't just burst in—' But Des was away to his
next venture, and she hadn't even discovered what his
mother was called or whether there was a father too.

Beside the lift doors a notice was mounted on a gilt easel,
'Main Lounge closed. Guests are respectfully invited to use
the Bars, Card Lounge, and Television Room.' Paula went
through to the Maze Bar and ordered an espresso. The
barman tonight was a lumbering bear with a heavily creased
face. 'You like Knossos Palace?' he inquired as he set down
her coffee. He must have assumed that she was on the coach
party that left after lunch. 'I didn't join today's excursion,'
she said truthfully.

He just nodded. 'Bus is better,' he agreed. 'No guide to
talk your head off.'

Paula relented. 'I went alone. I was very impressed.'

'Good, good. I work once in London. Buckingham Palace
is preddy too.'

The arrival of several of the Fiesta party saved her from
matching his compliment. Paula was relieved, not sure what
you could offer someone who found the Queen's London
residence 'preddy'. She made room for the four New Zealan-
ders, the Colonel and his Cynth, and a Junoesque blonde
in sequinned chiffon of midnight blue. On introduction she
learned that this was a Mrs Van Leiden.

'English, sweetie, not Dutch,' the lady explained. 'Not
even early New Yorkers, my late husband's lot. You must
be Des's new friend. You've made a great impression on
him. "Not bad, for a girl," he described you. Praise indeed.
He's a nascent misogynist, you know.'

'I didn't actually. He's good company.'

'As small boys go. Yes, well, what's everyone drinking?'

The women settled like a flock of vivid birds and began a pecking conversation, full of little cries of delight or amusement. They made swoops and darts at various topics, found them empty and tossed them away. Paula watched, mildly entertained.

Not so much birds, she appreciated after a few minutes; but more like women at a store sale, trying each other on for size, wriggling to find their own better angles. Perhaps because of Mrs Van Leiden's presence, which was considerable, the others seemed different from last night, almost competitive, larger than life. It was an age-span and a level of society she hadn't moved in much of late, and it made her more reticent.

'You're very silent, my dear,' the Colonel said suddenly, putting a hand lightly on her own. There was nothing familiar about the touch of his dry, paper-fine skin. His handsome old eyes showed only concern. 'I hope you've not overdone things today. In the sun.'

She assured him she'd had a lazy time and had already acclimatized herself on the mainland. 'I just take my pleasures quietly.'

'Very wise of you, my dear,' Cynth approved. 'Stanley, shall we all make one big table for dinner? Could you ask the *maître d'* to have two of them put together? It's always so much more fun, don't you think?' And then she added something under her breath, only for herself. Paula, startled, thought she'd whispered, 'So much safer too.'

'Look, Cynth,' said the Colonel, rock-steady, 'we're on holiday. You've got your pretty new dress on. It's all right.'

Mrs Van Leiden opened her blue eyes wider at the apparent irrelevance and there was an awkward pause in the conversation. Cynth looked down in her lap and plucked at the stuff of her skirt. Her hands fluttered then towards her husband. 'Yes, I have. But Stanley, it would be fun, wouldn't it? Us all together.'

'Splendid idea,' said Des's mother quickly.

Scott, the New Zealander, stood up. 'I'll go and fix it up with the dining-room, and see how soon dinner will be.'

In the event the table was set for ten. Des didn't put in an appearance, nor did Mrs Van L seem to expect him. When the Bowles couple came in as the others started on their soup, Gaynor Scott, the fluffy twin, raised a hand in greeting and they took it as an invitation. Melissa slid in beside Paula, and her husband sat opposite.

After their encounter of the afternoon the girl would have preferred not to meet the bold stare of his silver eyes. She turned towards Melissa and started to tell her about the film company. Mrs Van L took it up with an amusing account of their activities of the previous week. 'Wait until you see their leading lady. Too gorgeous to be true. An odalisque, straight from Omar Khayyam, or a Turkish Delight advertisement. She's Egyptian actually and accompanied by both parents; very arrogant, the father.'

'Not Muslim then,' Cynth murmured, 'or I doubt if they'd allow—'

'Oh, no danger there,' said Des's mother cheerfully. 'Her leading man's a eunuch.'

A little ripple of laughter went round the table, partly amused, partly uncomfortable.

Malcolm Bowles lifted his strange eyes and fixed them on Mrs Van Leiden. 'My dear lady,' he said with a drawling condescension unsuited to his years, 'how can you possibly tell without—?'

'Vibes,' she claimed with slangy confidence. 'I can tell one of those on sight.'

Paula considered her. This was the woman who had called the front desk manager 'The Prince of the Lilies'. It had annoyed her at the time, having found the fresco of the young Minoan peerless. If the woman was wrong about the one she could be wrong about the other. But what did she make of Malcolm Bowles himself?

It wasn't possible to be sure of her attitude. She was drinking from a wineglass, apparently unconscious of him now, yet Paula believed her moved by a sense of mischief.

Or not? Perhaps I misjudged the other situation, Paula thought. The two men could have met for some other furtive reason than the one she'd supposed. And the Bowles couple had arrived only last night. How long did it take for one to recognize another of his kind? Longer than it took to set up some illicit form of business deal? Because whatever the reason for their meeting, she had felt strongly that it had been deliberate and for some underhand and questionable purpose.

Give him the benefit of the doubt, Paula decided. Or at least check out that the person with him hadn't been his wife. Mightn't the other man have come along much as she did herself and then turned away? 'Did you enjoy Knossos?' she asked Melissa.

'Oh, I haven't been yet. Malcolm insisted I should rest. It was rather exciting yesterday, flying out from London. I must have been more tired than I thought, because I slept right through until six. And I still feel sleepy. We're going there tomorrow.'

So that confirmed that Melissa hadn't been the second dim shape in the South House, the one who giggled. And what's it to me? Paula considered. Each to his own hobby after all.

Melissa suddenly remembered that Paula was a student and wanted to guess her subject. 'You dress too smartly for an artist,' she judged. 'Music? But don't music students have to practise for hours each day, even on holiday?'

'You mean you can't see her double bass?' Michaela squawked from the table's far end. 'Takes it everywhere she—'

'Domestic Science,' Cynth said hopefully. 'You look as if you'd be a good cook. Stanley, wouldn't you say—?'

'Something more intellectually demanding, I think.

Thank goodness it's no longer considered rude to recognize when a woman's got brains.'

'Women are into everything now,' said Malcolm Bowles down his nose.

'I've just done a year at Law School,' Paula admitted. 'After University. The next stage is pupillage.' She smiled, aware that to outsiders it sounded regressive.

'Postgraduate? My, my.' Bowles was staring at her coldly.

'Malcolm's a solicitor,' Melissa announced proudly. 'A very clever one. He manages everything for me, and did for Uncle James.'

'Melissa, there are many sides to the Law. Miss—Miss Musto is possibly bound for a career in Criminal Law. Even the Bar.'

'Which is where we should move to for coffee and liqueurs,' Mrs Van Leiden interrupted. They all started to rise and push back their chairs. 'What *have* you done,' the same lady asked of Paula in an undertone, 'to upset that young man?'

'I've no idea.'

'I think you have.'

'Are you sure I've upset him?'

'Sweetie, if looks could kill—'

Paula wasn't going to pass on scandal, nor even own to finding her suspicions distasteful. She would forget having seen Bowles at Knossos, and he could do the same for her. But Mrs Van L was watching her shrewdly. 'He just thinks I saw something which I didn't quite.'

The woman snorted with laughter. 'Didn't you love what Melissa accidentally said—"He *did* for Uncle James"! I could just see it. Manual strangulation of a geriatric, or more likely the sneaky arsenic teabag. He's a nasty man, sweetie. You should watch your step.'

Paula smiled serenely. 'I usually do.'

On their way from the dining-room they passed the two nurses who shared a table with a couple she hadn't seen before, a heavily built elderly woman with iron-grey hair and a thin young man who was smiling into space. 'Who would they be?' Paula asked Des's mother when they had gone by.

'The Frau Doktor and her son Jozsef. Oh, what's she called? Müller, Brunner? No, Toller. His name's Kanski, which sounds Polish to me, but they could have Swiss or Austrian nationality. They come in for meals most days. I think they're long-stay visitors, in a rented apartment in the town somewhere.'

'I see. They were speaking French.'

'The Frau Doktor's a linguist, not a medico. Retired University type. You know how Middle Europeans throw their qualifications at you.'

The Maze Bar was already filling. The film crew had taken a break and were strung out on high stools along the counter. Their leading lady, who was all and more than she'd been described as, sat apart with her parents and a boy of about eight. As the Fiesta group split up to find places the child stood up, bowed formally to his father and went across to where Des was playing a Star Wars machine against the farther wall.

The English boy took no notice but completed his electronic mayhem, fired his last laser, scanned his score in disgust and turned away. The younger boy tugged at his arm and Des shook his head, reaching in his trouser pockets to pull the linings inside out. He made shooing gestures with his hands and the small boy stamped in rage.

'That child,' Mrs Van Leiden observed, 'is a stinking imp. Totally spoilt. Because his sister's fallen on her feet he expects everyone to pet him. Des is the only one here who dares give any backchat. Unfortunately the novelty of offhand treatment seems to attract the little beast.'

'Des can take care of himself.'

'I tell myself so.' Mrs Van Leiden looked unusually sombre. 'I let him take risks, for fear of smothering him. It isn't very comfortable sometimes when he's a long time away. But we do communicate in private. All I want is for him to grow up with some judgment and stand on his own feet.'

'Lucky Des. I was a widow's mite too, but rather more of an embarrassment. And expected to stay young.'

'It hasn't scarred you.'

Paula flushed. 'Don't think I wasn't fond of Mother. It's just that she was so transparent that it hurt rather. She was incredibly hopeful and trusting with every new man she met, and always unlucky in the end. I even thought once how much better if God had left my father and taken her. The two of us would have managed our life together so much better.'

'And now?'

'We've both survived. She's alive and arthritic and living on Jersey. We usually meet twice a year, when she's painfully apologetic and wonders why I'm not married to a rich young husband. I could never explain to her.'

'She's afraid of your detachment,' Mrs Van Leiden assumed swiftly. 'As I would be in her place. Formidable young lady. Probably that's how our Mr Bowles sees you. He cares so much what other people see him as, and you don't. He thinks you see right through him.'

'What do you make of Melissa?'

'More of a ward than a wife,' said the forthright lady. 'I ask myself, is she rich? Will she still be, ten years from now? I've a horrid, suspicious mind, haven't I?'

'No worse than mine. You say aloud the things I think to myself. Perhaps we're bad for each other.'

'Whatever we are, I'm going up now to play bridge. Why don't you come along and watch, if you won't play? At least it's quieter than here.'

The bar being overcrowded by this point, Paula followed along to watch Mrs Van Leiden partnering Colonel Martin against Mr Scott and Mildred Pallett. Beyond them was a

high-spirited quartet known as the Canadian Widows, short
on forgiveness for sloppy bidding and long on Metaxa
brandy, lacquered hair-dos and eye-catching jewellery. The
play generally was less interesting than the people involved,
but when after a couple of rubbers Paula was aware that
across the room the phoney RAF moustache was twitching
at her, in association with a left eye which rapidly disappeared several times in porcine wrinkles of flesh, she opted
to escape. Gaynor Scott had looked in to say that the filming
was over and the lounge cleared for dancing, so Paula joined
those who drifted in that direction.

The arc lights had been replaced by the room's normal
dusky suggestiveness. A stereo tape-player churned out
disco pulp from one corner under the dipping fronds of
potted palms and oleanders. The gorgeous odalisque was
exotically gyrating for an elderly Arab, her parents looking
on. Gaynor Scott limply flapped her arms and pushed at
the floor without lifting her feet, distantly partnered by
the film's male cast. Her twin Michaela was engaged in
conversation with a large, overweight Irishman between
thirty and forty. He had moistly pallid skin, a long cow-
catcher upper lip and the dull, flat-eyed gaze of a drunk.

'Don' you wanna be a filmstar?' he asked complainingly.
'What're you doin' that's better than that?'

Michaela gave him her abrupt sideways look over one
shoulder. It was the bare one. The other one was stiff with
ruchings of black taffeta and puce net. The skirt of her
Dali-like dress ended above one knee and dipped in a spiky
train behind the other. Tonight her make-up was more
bizarre than ever.

'In fact,' she said, deadpan but making erotic movements
with her neck and torso, 'I'm a brain surgeon. And you
fascinate me—professionally.'

'I do?' He was swaying on his feet and took a few stumbling steps after her as Michaela twitched out of reach,
angular and monkey-malicious, intent on drawing him.

'He is a good sound-recordist,' apologized a lithe, dark-haired man beside Paula. 'Can I get you an ice or a drink?'

'No, thank you. I've not long had dinner.'

'My name is Franco Ferri,' he said formally, 'and it is my company that makes the film and disturbs your comfort here. Will you forgive me and dance a little?'

He seemed pleasant enough and quite willing to tell her about his present project. He had had some early success in Rome recording small music groups in partnership with the Irishman, but his ambition had always been to make films. With his first movie camera he launched a company producing TV ads for which his friend wrote the jingles. The profit from this allowed him to expand to his present team of eight technicians using two cameras, although for veracity he was opposed to alternating viewpoints, 'because we each have only one pair of eyes, one response, one judgment.'

'So what kind of films are you making now?' Paula asked him.

Franco had a baroque smile. He shook his head and the black curls tumbled on his forehead. 'Vanity films. Films for people who want everyone to see them. It is like poets who pay to have their own works published.'

'Do you mean that the lovely girl we saw—'

'Is living out her fantasy, yes. She is very lovely, as you say. But no actress. And she has a rich friend, an Arab, who has a fancy to finance her. Which is convenient for us all. Even such a film can be well directed, well scripted and edited. So all the time I travel a little farther. One day I get real actors, make a great film.'

'I somehow feel you will.' Their dance ended and they found seats in a window that opened on to the night. A lighted plane was throbbing overhead, dropping towards Iraklion airport. Only last night it had been her turn to arrive. 'I do like it here,' Paula said impulsively, 'although it's not what I expected.'

She looked round the room at the dancers, the drinkers and the sitters-out. She had happened on a very mixed set of people, but already they began to belong together, and she with them. Tomorrow there was an excursion to the east corner of the island, to Elounda, Aghios Nikolaos and Kritsa. She decided to add her name to the list on the noticeboard.

'But this isn't Crete,' Franco said, meaning the hotel. 'I should like to take you walking down to the harbour, if it would not be impertinent to ask.'

She smiled. Andy Whitelaw had been so adamant that there was no crime on Crete, and anyway the night being stifling indoors without air-conditioning, the streets were full of local people. Safety in numbers, even with a stranger. 'I should like a walk,' she accepted.

She was glad she had decided in favour. Franco was charming and correct, and the city by night was an altogether more vivacious and sensual place than in daytime. There was plenty to watch on the waterfront, and rewarding glimpses of *taverna* life as they strolled back by the narrow streets. All was velvet, warm and pleasant until the sudden, chilling end.

They approached the hotel from its rear and in the shadows of one end of the flagged terrace were two or three people in a group, one kneeling.

'Signorina, please stay here. There is something wrong.'

Franco went forward but Paula was close behind. 'No,' he said, trying to shield the scene from her eyes. 'There has been an accident. Someone has fallen from a balcony.

'It seems to be the boy. He is dead.'

CHAPTER 8

Nobody shouted or ran off, but the little knot of onlookers was suddenly reinforced by hotel staff, then passers-by.

'We can do nothing,' Franco said calmingly and drew her away.

Paula needed his steadying arm. The abrupt change from harmony to horror had shattered her. Twenty-four hours back it would have shocked her less because then she hadn't met Des, hadn't listened while his outwardly carefree mother admitted her concern: still tragic, a young life wasted, but something that happened to strangers. Now, having shared that empathy, she felt her own security threatened.

Franco steered her by the elbow. The Maze Bar was shuttered and no one on duty. 'In my room,' he said, 'I have cognac. It will take no time to fetch it. Sit here, please.'

He brought as well a severely masculine dressing-gown of fine wool which he draped round her shoulders. With its warmth and the fire of the brandy she found her shuddering passed. 'I'm sorry. You're so kind.'

'Sudden death.' He nodded. 'And the boy so young.'

'I knew him,' she explained. 'How on earth could it have happened?'

'We may know soon. The police and a medical team have arrived. They will be asking questions. I'm afraid they will need to see you before you retire.'

'I couldn't sleep now in any case.'

Already the newcomers were spreading through the hotel, issuing instructions. There were two kinds of uniform: the Tourist Police and some hard-eyed men who made concessions to no one. Franco and Paula made statements separately and these were checked against each other, their watches examined to verify times. 'I can't be exact,' Paula admitted. 'There was no reason to keep to a schedule.'

'I had the lounge cleared by eleven-seventeen,' Franco detailed. 'I met Miss Musto at about eleven-thirty-two. We left for our walk ten minutes later. I am very conscious how time passes, because of my work. So much of filming is a question of planning time and space.'

The policeman looked at them both coldly. An *Italian*, he was probably thinking, and his English pick-up. At last the quick anger which overtook Paula started to crowd out the horror. 'Mrs Van Leiden,' she asked the policeman, 'where is she?'

'Van Leiden?'

'The boy's mother. I should go to her. Please!

'Oh no,' Franco began, but the policeman silenced him with a brief gesture. 'What room number?'

'I've no idea. The register—'

They were interrupted by the arrival of a more senior policeman who conferred in rapid Greek.

'Ah,' said their interviewer, 'one more question. When were you both last on the roof?'

Paula stared at him. The *roof*? But the boy had fallen from his balcony. Hadn't he? The man repeated his question impatiently and she tried to think back. 'This morning. I swam before breakfast. That is, yesterday morning, I suppose.'

Franco's turn. 'I was up there last Friday. We were filming beside the pool. I haven't been there since.'

'Why the roof?' Paula managed to get in.

The senior policeman gazed at her blankly. 'Because although the boy's room is at the rear of the hotel, it was not above where he fell. So he came from someone else's balcony, or the roof.'

'But the roof's perfectly safe, unless he climbed over the—'

'Exactly. Or was thrown over.'

She wouldn't believe it. There were limits even to nightmares. 'Not *Des*!' she said fiercely.

'No.' Franco put his hand on her arm. 'I tried to tell you. *Not* Des. It was the other boy. Muna's little brother Sayid.'

One effect of the tragedy was to bring the group closer, Paula found. Once she knew that the dead boy wasn't Des but an outsider she could relax. And was ashamed of her new lack of feeling. This unknown boy had a mother too, and friends. The family must be distraught. She caught no glimpse of them. By breakfast time, when all the versions of the night's events were being competitively swapped and edited by the Fiesta members, the stricken family had moved out.

Franco appeared briefly to take his leave of Paula, courteous and concerned as ever. There could be no more filming now. He made no mention of keeping in touch but hoped that sometime their paths would cross again. Which was all she wanted.

In a brave attempt at lifting her own spirits she put on the tangerine skirt and black top. (The black a subconscious concession to a death?) Joining the others awaiting their coach on the hotel steps, she found herself swept into the boisterous company of the Canadian Widows, like macaws with their harsh, confident voices and vivid colours. One, hailing her as 'Tangerine' because of the skirt, kept a seat for her in the coach. Her name was Kate and she came from Toronto, a frank and drily witty woman, the ideal pick-me-up in such circumstances.

It saved the day for her, and when she next saw the Van Leidens on her return, all she felt was impatience at her own confusion of the body's identity. There was no grisly reminder to be seen of last night's disaster. The hotel had sanitized the entire incident. Sad and final, but over.

Anyone who was so indiscreet as to refer to it again was told that the boy had been uncontrollable and climbed over the barrier to fetch a quoit, which daylight had revealed on the outer coping.

In private Paula confessed to Mrs Van Leiden the searing mistake she'd made when Franco said, 'It's the boy!'

'Des isn't so foolhardy as that, to go after a quoit in the dark,' said his mother, not heatedly but as though her thoughts were elsewhere. 'Actually he did go up to the roof garden. He told me so. It was just before midnight. He was looking for you. He thought you might take a swim before bed.'

'Could the other boy have followed him up, do you think?'

'I wondered that. He was in dark pyjamas, but no one seems to have seen him on the way up. He must have been put to bed by their maid and then sneaked out while she was busy elsewhere.'

'His parents would have been chaperoning Muna as usual.'

'Apparently not.' The woman's tone was dry. 'Des caught a glimpse of her on the roof with her Arab. They were arguing pretty hotly, he said. They never saw him because he kept the air-conditioning shaft between. He made a wide circuit to the pool, saw it was empty and came back below. He didn't get to bed until midnight, which is far too late, but it's holiday after all, and he was asleep in no time.'

'Did he tell the police this?'

'Oh yes, and the damned girl denied it flatly. Afraid of losing face before Papa, I suppose. Fortunately she has the reputation of being a congenital liar, but the police came back and cross-questioned Des again. They seemed to think the two boys might have been playing together and had a fight, or Des dared the younger one to go out over the edge. The trouble is that Des just clams up when he thinks no one believes him. It rests, I think, with the police hoping an eye-witness will turn up. Otherwise it will be written off as an accident pure and simple. Which is the version the hotel would prefer, stressing the perversity of the boy in flouting safety regulations.'

'Cretans aren't exactly safety-conscious. Look at all those unlit piles of sand on pavement edges, even sheets of glass left leaning against shop walls in the dark.'

'No, but they go through the motions of being bothered, when tourists are involved. They'll do all they can to blacken the poor child.'

'You did say Sayid was a little stinker.'

'Small consolation to be proved right in this way. God, I feel for his mother!'

Forget it, Paula told herself. She shouldn't have mentioned her fears to Mrs Van L. Unknown small boys were dying all over the world, and it went on turning. This was a holiday.

She started describing the day's excursion, the *al fresco* lunch at Aghios Nikolaos, the hauntingly sad, wide-eyed Byzantine saints of the faded frescoes at Kritsa.

Recognizable groups were forming among the Fiesta travellers. Notably there was what Paula thought of as the Metaxa-Bridge Zealots. This comprised the phoney RAF moustache, the man's equally large and brash sister and her peripheral husband, a mild, jaded businessman-turned-publican from somewhere in the Midlands. Their fourth member varied according to circumstances, often being Mildred Pallett—or was it Muriel? Paula had twice mistakenly addressed her as Miriam, and once as Millicent, which hadn't advanced her popularity with the lady. Regrettable, but the woman was so unremarkable that to Paula one name seemed as likely as another.

Then there were the Canadian Widows, who thought of themselves as The Whoopee Girls, so independent that their numbers fluctuated between three and six according to occasion. One or another of them was forever dashing off by taxi to far corners of the island or holding protracted bargaining sessions with local shopkeepers, particularly jewellers. Their numbers were supplemented at times by the appearance for bridge of Mr Foden, the Englishman Paula had met in the café on the Square, on her first day here. He would acknowledge her with a quizzical nod, and watching him she discovered that the man had two exteriors; one dour and uncommunicative when stone sober, and quite another when he had been drinking. Then he was prepared to find certain individuals acceptable enough as card-players while he withered them with his scalding wit. His was a personality to be reckoned with, and Paula was curious to know more about him.

The Runcorn widow's pursuit of Ben Kimber was by now the subject of a book made by the phoney RAF moustache, and he was offering high odds. The Yorkshireman was smugly allowing her advances, adding interest to the chase by a vague appearance of attraction in alternative directions. He'd done little more than glance at the younger of the two nurses, who found his accent difficult to penetrate, made the odd sortie with various other unattached ladies and was regularly seen drinking at the expense of Gaynor Scott. Of her twin sister he was noticeably wary, recognizing Michaela as astute beyond her years and altogether in a class of her own. At such times, while he played the field, Ella Sharp stomped doggedly round alone, red notebook at the ready, absorbing fresh information to enrich his interest when he should return to her side.

There was also a new friendship being forged which Paula thought of as the Unholy Alliance. The Frau Doktor Toller and her son were now to be seen at every meal with Irène Petitjean and Sylvie Audoin. Paula, questioning why she could have hit on such a label, decided it was because she doubted the degree of friendship and also its motives. There were convenient reasons for the grouping, of course, such as the languages. Few of the English-speaking visitors had much French, but the Frau Doktor was more than fit to cope. Jozsef too was fluent, when he felt disposed for conversation. It was perhaps his mother's determined bid for the other two that Paula found inexplicable, unless it was because they were nurses. Frau Toller was perhaps a hypochondriac?

Idly Paula put the supposition to Foden, that cynical observer of the human scene, whom she joined at his table in the late sunshine of Eleftherías Square. He grunted from under the linen hat which covered his eyes.

'That solid lady? Never. Try the son. Look at him.'

Paula looked. He seemed so abstracted, so untouched by all that went on around him that she had barely considered him. Now she questioned the faint, dreamy smile, the lanky, indolent frame, with the bony wrists and ankles hanging out beyond his off-the-peg summer suit. Its material was good but it had been bought in a hurry and not altered to fit. His mother's dresses too—she was never seen in trousers—looked expensive but lacked style. She had a heavily fleshed, unbending body, went barelegged in open-toed sandals, and the darkness at her thick ankles could equally well have been small broken veins or ingrained grime.

No, Foden was right. The lady was too stolid and unimaginative to be a health-faddist. So perhaps it *was* Jozsef, because there was some grim purpose in the way Frau Toller reached for the pair of nurses.

'Second full day,' Paula wrote that night in her diary, listing the things done, and deliberately left blank Thursday's half-page before it which she had been too tired to fill in, stumbling to bed after the police questioning on the little boy's death fall.

It was the following morning, Saturday, when she was leaving the hotel and the lift failed, that Paula understood what Foden had seen and she had missed.

The space was cramped. Paula had got in on her top floor with an American in a towelling robe who'd come from the roof garden. On the third floor there were four people waiting, but the Frau Doktor and Jozsef had only been visiting the nurses and were being seen off. The women stood back as the lift filled. It went down another floor but the door failed to open. Someone outside banged on it to no avail. The American clucked and put his finger on the button marked Ground Floor. The lift started off, stopped, restarted, juddered, and went out of action midway between the second and third floors. The four of them were plunged in darkness.

There were the usual tetchy comments. The American hit the alarm button. He started on a long story about a 'shack' hotel in Austria where he'd been marooned in a shaft for eight hours. Towards its end they heard someone calling down from above, in Greek.

'Try English, dammit,' the American bawled back, then looked at the others pugnaciously. 'We all talk English here?'

'We do,' agreed the Frau Doktor.

Paula now had the opportunity to appreciate her at close quarters. She was in fact a little too close. The lady was well-built, with a full, dowagerlike bust. It pressed into Paula's shoulder as they eased themselves into fresh positions. She realized that the woman was making more room for her son. A dim emergency light came on and she saw him leaning back against the long mirror in the rear, frowning and staring wildly.

'Is he all right?' Paula murmured.

'I think so, for the moment.'

'Perhaps he should sit down.' Already it was a little late. A spasm crossed his face and the eyes rolled upwards. There was a soft drumming as his rubber heels vibrated on the lift floor. His body shook.

'Quiet!' the American commanded, his back turned to them. 'I can't hear what the guy's saying.'

Paula had never seen an epileptic seizure, but guessed it was that. Together with his mother she lowered the young man gently to the floor. His hands clutched and contracted over hers. The trembling passed over into her body.

It wasn't very violent, and was soon over. Throughout it, Frau Toller remained prosaically calm. Jozsef lay between their feet, his long legs bent up in the confined space, his cheek on Paula's silk cravat that she'd torn from the neck of her blouse. His mother grunted. 'It is not bad. He was already sedated.' She began talking him round quietly in German.

When his eyes opened he saw Paula kneeling alongside and seemed puzzled. Perhaps because he had been talking French with the two nurses just before, he used it to her. '. . . *suis tombé?*'

She smiled. '*Evidemment. Rien de sérieux.*' She took her hand from his grip and rose to her feet, brushing at her skirt.

There was a sound of winding as some mechanism came into operation above. The lift creaked and started moving very slowly. When it stopped again the doors clicked and came open. The whole mishap had taken no more than ten minutes.

'Please continue in the other lift,' the duty manager said, waiting outside. They transferred in beside two strangers, Paula's hand supporting Jozsef's arm. He could bear his own weight but remained bemused.

Instead of down, the lift went up. The American groaned, then shrugged. 'What the hell. It's a holiday.'

'My floor,' Paula told the other two. 'Do come in and sit down for a while. I'll ring down to have some coffee sent in.'

'You are a kind girl,' the woman said. 'And sensible. I am very grateful.'

'I'm called Paula, Frau Doktor.'

'No formality, please. I am Magda, if I do not seem too old for you to use it. This is my son, Jozsef.'

While they waited for the coffee Paula folded back the duvet and nodded Jozsef towards the bed. 'Just rest for a moment. We'll be out on the balcony if you need us.' She half closed the slatted shutter behind her, so that it left the room shaded and cool.

Frau Toller—Magda, as she must call her—was leaning over the ornate railing, looking down the face of the building. 'This is near where that poor child fell?' Her English was almost accentless, but then languages had been her profession.

Paula stood beside her. 'It's the same side of the hotel, but it was farther along. Here the trees might have broken his fall. Unfortunately it was over the terrace, just beyond the steps.'

'You saw it happen then?'

'We came across it, just after. I never exactly *saw* him.'

'An only son. Terrible.' She stood dejected, feeling a mother's grief, picturing it as her own. 'Children make us vulnerable. It is wonderful to have them, but it is then that we see—how bad the world is.'

Paula felt helpless. It would have been presumptuous to reach out and touch her. It was clear that the old lady had been the victim of earlier disasters but was an indomitable survivor.

'Have you other children?' she ventured.

'Only Jozsef. There were difficulties when he was born. He suffered some brain damage, only slight, and I could have no more children. It was in 1956. But I managed to get over the border just in time. Jozsef was born in Austria.'

Paula thought quickly. 1956. 'The Hungarian Rising?'

'We were Magyars, yes. Rising? I am not sure that is the right word. To you it sounds like rebellion. It *was* a rising in another sense; that we felt an enormous, sudden hope, an uplift of spirit, because Stalinism was dead and the old ways losing their hold.'

She moved back into one of the cane armchairs and Paula put a cushion behind her shoulders. 'Thank you. Hope is a dangerous amphetamine. Some of us earlier had seen salvation in the Nazis, because we did need discipline, and protection from our neighbours. I was still at school then, in Budapest, my father a banker. Suddenly I discovered that many of our friends were Jewish. I hadn't noticed it before. They disappeared. But my own family were safe, acceptable so long as we did not step out of line. But in welcoming Nazi help against the Serbs we also inherited their enemies. It was a long war. I grew up while it was on, studied, took my first degree, and then the Russians came. In their turn they were the dawn hope of our revolutionary workers and peasants, but the New Order was chaos for such as us. My father was disgraced and ruined, my older brother shot by the political police. Little Kareli died on the Eastern Front. Those who prospered under the Communists were vindictive and made it hard for their old masters. I— was abused at first, as a young woman, but then I found work out in the country on a farm, like one of my uncle's old peasants, but without the protection they had known. But the bureaucrats found me out and made me return to Buda to work for them. They needed translators. Already I spoke Hungarian, German, French. I was adding English, and picked up some Russian from the advisers they sent us. But I was not trusted, because of my origins. So I married a Party man who befriended me, to be safe. We were not unhappy together. His name was Jozsef, and so eventually I gave his son that name. Don't imagine he was named after Stalin!'

'And in 1956?'

'Jozsef was as deceived as many other of our leaders. We had been occupied since '45, but when Stalin died in '53 we saw Russian oppression slowly loosen its hold. We know now that they were too busy to notice us, being preoccupied with power struggles for his successor, and that endless Korean war. Overlooked, we might have achieved some discreet approach to independence, but there was too much joy in our release, and such euphoria scared our old hard-liners who appealed to Moscow. The Kremlin seemed almost ready to make some concessions, but then Nagy went too far. He spoke of neutrality, even a break with the Warsaw Pact. That was too much for our masters. Russia sent in its tanks.'

She stopped talking, lost in memories of long-past horrors. Then she smiled bitterly. 'We saw then that our hope had been empty all along. It was a choice of stand and be destroyed or run for your life. Jozsef could not accept this. He was one of a group of comrades who went out to reason with the tank crews in Parliament Square. Machine-guns opened fire on them from the roofs. It was claimed that rebels did it, because some of the Russians were killed, but we knew who held all those buildings. The tanks started firing indiscriminately. They rode over everyone. Hundreds were massacred, and among them Jozsef.'

She moved in her chair. 'I was sickened. I was thirty-three and carrying my first child. I wanted the whole world for him, a free world. So I made my way out. I packed a small bag, begged a lift into the countryside and started to walk to the frontier. Seven months pregnant, and the November snows due. There is not much I remember of those two weeks, but I am here. My child was born in freedom and is now a man. If sometimes he has this weakness I know who to blame. And still there is much to be glad of.'

'You married again.'

'A good man, an Austrian. A professor at the University where I obtained a junior lectureship. I had arrived empty-handed but not empty-brained. Education is hard to destroy, almost as hard as a sense of family. I can never forget whose daughter I was, or who Jozsef is descended from. We were lucky, because I married a man who had no one. When he died, five years ago, I inherited his estates, and having worked in the Hungarian vineyards I knew enough to manage them. My son has healthy work outdoors and has studied viticulture. We have made a success of the venture.'

'A triumph of endurance.'

The woman gave a harsh bark of grim laughter. 'As you say. But what of Jozsef? I have to think about him, make plans for his protection.'

'Yes, I see.' Paula thought she understood quite a lot about the woman now, certainly her motive for the 'Unholy Alliance'. Whatever the two nurses had to gain in the unlikely foursome, Frau Toller was picking their brains, extracting medical information on recent treatments for epilepsy. Could Jozsef's be the case Irène had been discussing when Paula eavesdropped in the coach and guessed their profession? The Sister had been minimizing the young man's condition to Sylvie, almost persuasively. Her practised eye would have diagnosed it on first meeting. Even Paula herself had thought him strangely languid. Phenobarbitone was still used for epilepsy, wasn't it? Some drug anyway that acted as a damper, put a baffle on excitement for an over-sensitized brain.

She crossed to the balcony shutter and looked into the dim room. Jozsef lay at full length on the bed. Asleep he looked young and defenceless. It was almost the same situation as with Des and his mother, but more poignant.

There was a knock at the door and a waiter came in with their coffee. It was the massive bearlike one who had served her the first evening and known she'd taken the bus to Knossos. As he found a surface for the tray, Jozsef began stirring.

'For three,' the waiter said woodenly.

'Three is correct.' Frau Toller came in from the balcony and Paula had to hide her smile. The woman was concerned about propriety, determined that Paula should not be gossiped about. Doubtless she had reason. Hotels on Crete weren't like those in sophisticated London where such situations were expected.

'Jozsef, it is time for your medication.'

'I suppose so, but I feel quite well now.' He had a slow, shy smile and his voice was pleasant.

'Nevertheless . . .' His mother retrieved a small bottle from her handbag and tipped out a tablet on to his saucer. He directed a droll grimace at Paula and obediently swallowed the medicine.

'I do apologize for my absence,' he said. 'I hope it was not too great an embarrassment.'

'These things happen,' Paula commented easily. 'I'm glad you're feeling better.' She didn't find it easy to talk to him with his mother listening, which was a pity because, as well as feeling sympathy, she liked him. There was a frankness, a complete lack of challenge about him which appealed to her. 'You don't live in the hotel, I believe.'

They told her about their rooms in the Old Town, very island-Greek and simple. They had been there three weeks already and found their neighbours very pleasing. 'I wish I had some of them to work for me,' Jozsef said surprisingly. 'It is a pity that such good people produce such indifferent wine. It is because the sun is too hot.'

It set them off on a new tack, swapping the names on printed labels. 'What have you been drinking here?' Jozsef asked.

'Samaina,' Paula told him, reaching inside the wardrobe for a bottle. 'I found it in the market. It's a little drier than the other Samos wines. The hotel doesn't stock it, though.'

'You could try their Minos for a local wine. It is not good, but it goes with the food well. A wine is essential, because of the grease.' He had forgotten his malaise, was almost vivacious.

'Have you seen a lot of the island in your three weeks?' Paula asked. 'Tell me what I mustn't miss. I've so little time. Only until Wednesday.'

They inquired what places she had already visited and suggested enough for a full month's stay; villages where special crafts were followed; spectacular views; neolithic caves; Minoan sites. 'With a hire-car and driver,' Frau

Toller said, accepting a refill of coffee, 'one can go where one fancies. Perhaps,' she added, 'you would let us repay your hospitality by being our guest one day? Unfortunately you have not long here and we already have made some arrangements—'

With the nurses, Paula guessed. That would be what they were getting out of the alliance: free transport to places of interest.

'Perhaps,' Jozsef suggested, 'we could change some of the arrangements, put them off to next week?'

His mother stared hard at him. 'You really wish that?'

'Certainly.'

'Then I will see what I can do, Jozsef. Miss—Paula, I hope you can find time to come exploring with us?'

'I hope so too. It's very kind of you.'

There was an exchange of thanks and formal compliments before they took their leave. Jozsef bowed his long frame and gave a slow smile. '*Auf wiedersehen, Fräulein.*'

'*Au revoir, Jozsef.*'

The Frau Doktor actually smiled at their poaching on her preserves. Paula stood a moment after they'd gone, considering, then darted a glance at her watch. Forty-seven minutes gone. If she left now she might just catch the later bus to Fódele.

CHAPTER 9

As Irène Petitjean let herself into the room she shared with Sylvie Audoin, she could smell cigarette smoke. 'Sylvie?'

There was an answering call from the balcony. She pushed the shutter back and went through to where the younger nurse was sprawled in a bikini, her shoulders and upper arms prawn pink. At least she'd had the sense to shade her face. She looked up now from under her floppy hat. 'Irène, can you pat some lotion on for me? I can't reach to where it's hurting.'

'You'll never tan properly. You have the wrong kind of skin. People like you just go red,' Irène insisted. 'Putting that stuff on is like basting meat. You end as pork crackling.'

Sylvie looked up at her resentfully. 'You are in a bad temper, Irène. What's wrong?'

'*You* are what's wrong! Anyone would think you have nothing to work for. You leave everything to me.'

'Because you get on better with the old woman. I never know what to talk to her about.'

'And how do you progress with her precious Jozsef? No, don't tell me. I'll tell you. They are not so enchanted, either of them. In fact I have just seen her and she wants to postpone some outings until next week. It is because of the English girl. It seems that she is setting her cap at your poor Jozsef. If so, you may kiss your chances goodbye, unless you make some real effort to be charming. It is fortunate the girl has only until Wednesday, and we stay on another week.'

'A fortnight's not long enough,' Sylvie complained. 'Not even long enough to look round properly.'

'We have looked,' the Sister Tutor said tartly, 'or, rather, I have done the looking for you. There is no one but Jozsef Kanski. That smug little Englishman Kimber is only playing at being available. I know his kind—the professional bachelor. He spends all he earns on himself. On holiday the women pay his bills. He'd be a fool to marry, and he knows it very well.

'Then there is the fluffy-moustached one who lives for his brandy and playing bridge. He has already arranged his life to suit himself, as parasite on his sister's marriage. There is no other unattached man who could provide the substantial background you're looking for. Anyway, Jozsef is entirely suitable. You know she throws her money about; it means nothing to them. You've seen photographs of where they live. All that land! Really, I envy you the chance. If I were still your age—'

'I'm not sure I want to tie myself to an invalid.'

'That is what makes it so suitable, so easy for you. Because you're a trained nurse, able to take care of him after his mother's gone. Sylvie Audoin, you are a fool! Take a look at yourself in the bathroom mirror. You're no Miss World who can choose from a list of millionaires. Capitalize on what you have, your usefulness in this case, or you may lose your last chance.'

'But an epileptic! That's all I'm good enough for? Maybe sometime I would want children.'

'You never said so before. Well, go ahead and have some. His is not an inherited strain. It was damage at birth. I've been all through it with the mother, and it's a disability I'm quite familiar with. There's little wrong with him. Regular medication keeps it to a minimum. His control would be Carbamazepine, something like that. Perfectly straightforward, nothing to bother him or you. If you ask me, his mother is over-anxious. If he hasn't married before, it's because she keeps him too close to her.'

Sylvie was looking stubborn and it didn't make her any more attractive. 'Well, take his mother. I don't get on with her, and she thinks I'm a fool. Suppose I marry Jozsef and something happens to him. If he died, where would I be? She's the one with the money, you said. I'd be no better off. Worse, really, because I'd have to crawl to her for my keep.'

'You're just making difficulties. If I'm to be your marriage-broker, which is how we arranged it, I shall naturally insist on a fair and independent settlement for you. And a respectable fee for my services, you may be sure. Since you will be the one to pay that, you will need resources, won't you? If you have lost confidence in my ability, just say so. We can go our own ways. God knows, I can find other ways to spend my holidays than in your company.'

'Oh Irène, don't be like that. Of course I have confidence

in you. It's just that the nearer I get to having to make up my mind—'

'Cold feet,' the older nurse said contemptuously. Well, she wasn't going to sing the praises of the married state. God knows she had suffered enough herself from falling into that trap, infatuated by a handsome face and persuasive tongue, not to mention a lithe and sexually dextrous body. Sylvie didn't know how lucky she was not to be troubled by passion. An arranged match was so much safer. In any case, this would probably be her only chance to reach the status she seemed to regard as her end in life.

Irène stripped, put away her street dress carefully—one of Sylvie's least lovely habits was the way she dropped her soiled clothes around—and pulled on her scarlet swimsuit. Lean and fleshless as she had stayed ever since her twenties, Irène's was not a figure that needed to be hidden in wraps on her way to the pool. She let herself out again into the corridor and walked the single flight up to the top floor, her towel with dark glasses and a paperback swinging in her tote bag. When she had found a space among the sunbathers, staked a claim and swum ten lengths of the pool she stretched out on her back in the sun. The book was to cover her face, not to read. She had no time to spare for reading, with so much else on her mind.

She marvelled how unexpectedly well it had turned out for that silly little staff nurse. Back in the autumn when, in an untypically patient moment, she had let her unburden herself, snivelling about her disappointments professional and personal, Irène had had no idea how she might eventually profit from the girl's pathetic wish to find herself a husband. One accepted that, basically, ninety-nine per cent of all women wanted to try matrimony or its near equivalent once in their lifetime, but actually to admit to another woman that you wanted it so much and yet didn't know how to go about it—that was abysmal!

For some reason, mildly amused exasperation perhaps,

she had seen fit to pretend sympathy. Later, after she'd had that first mind-shattering note from Zeid and had cast about her desperately for some means to take advantage of his unbelievable offer, she had remembered the girl. The idea had really come together of itself, a way to cover her need to travel south far enough for Zeid to risk contacting her. It had to be Crete, separated from Libya by only two hundred miles of sea.

There weren't many tours advertised in the Belgian press for the southern islands of Greece, but she'd found one in a London paper which a patient had brought in. Friendship International sounded slightly suspect, having a ring of political involvement to it, but its brochure, which she sent for, hadn't mentioned youth movements or any activity other than travel for pure enjoyment. Greece was obviously where the better-off British, Germans and Americans were going now, since Spain was too popular. People who sought a less commercial atmosphere, who were sufficiently educated to look out for archæological sites and classical remains were the sort little Sylvie Audoin romantically imagined her future belonged among. It hadn't been difficult to sell her the idea, a holiday with a deeper purpose. Between them they would make a contact which later could be built on with correspondence and visits. Subsequently, as in the stupid pulp romances on sale at every bookstall, a bee-ootiful relationship would blossom.

If Sylvie had swallowed the notion, she had certainly remained sceptical herself. Because the girl was such a *load*, so ungifted, and having so little to offer once you got past the quite modern cuteness of her features. Inhibited too, thanks to her puritanical upbringing. Even the practical aspects of male-ward nursing hadn't raised any normal urges in her.

'*Elle veut tout simplement se faire appeler Madame*,' Irène had explained to her flatmate Jeannine. Well, if Sylvie did actually (luck being in her favour) marry Jozsef Kanski,

Austrian citizen, she would get herself called '*Frau*' instead of '*Madame*', but it boiled down to the same thing.

Jeannine had accepted Irène's reason for making the trip, though she couldn't see why Irène should go to such trouble, even for a fee. Perhaps Jeannine had guessed that Sylvie didn't stand much chance anyway, once the swain got to know her. Then, of course, the fee wouldn't be forthcoming. 'Oh, it's a bit of a joke,' Irène had passed it off. 'The girl's got it into her head that she'll find her fate on Crete. I don't mind a fortnight in the sun at a discount. Who would?'

Which Jeannine had finally accepted, and Irène had no intention of confiding to her or to anyone her real reason for making the journey, any more than anyone back in Belgium had known of her early personal tragedy during three years' nursing in Lebanon. She had tried to forget it herself, knowing that there was nothing she could do to alter the outcome. Until Zeid's letter.

Even he, at the end, had come to see how impossible the results of his actions were. Not that she trusted him even now. He was a practised deceiver even as a young lover. Now, the matured vulpine features, the hard sinewy body advertised the ruthlessness of purpose and the callous disregard of a man whose only principles were political ones. Meeting him here, after so long a time, had been a terrible experience compounded of so many emotions that she had felt physically ill afterwards and could sleep only after downing half a bottle of brandy. Not a cure to be repeated if she needed to use her wits against him at any point, because he was cruelly twisted.

It did not astonish her at all that when he finally left Lebanon he should move to Libya. From gun-runner he had gone on to kidnapper and hired assassin. But even then, vile as he'd become, it seemed he still had mercy enough to want a better world for his—for *their*—daughter, snatched from her care seventeen years ago when Irène rebelled against the murderous nature of his secret life. A life so secret that there was no legal redress that could reach him, no way to trace the kidnapped baby.

To see Tammam again, to offer her the home that was rightly hers, to regain for her the right to Belgian nationality through her mother, that was all that mattered now, the one ambition left to a disillusioned woman approaching middle-age who had reached the peak of her career and learned to trust very few outside herself and to love no one. Tammam, the breathtakingly beautiful, dark-eyed baby, now nearly nineteen years of age!

Zeid had promised a photograph and she waited impatiently for its appearance in the mail. He'd said, softening momentarily, that Tammam was enchanting, willowy and courageous, but that he could no longer protect her as she needed. It was dangerous in the extreme to attempt to smuggle her out of Libya, but that was her only chance of liberation, of happiness. He had given much thought to it and to how it might be accomplished. The way he could best cover himself, and leave no tracks for the girl to be followed by, was if he used as agent the least likely person —his repudiated and discredited foreign wife. But even then, back in Belgium, she could not openly declare who the girl was, for fear of cruel reprisals. It was up to Irène to get her established there under cover, until such time as he could make a visit there on one of his missions for Qaddafi. Once there, she stood a better chance of getting authentic-looking identity papers. Meanwhile . . .

Meanwhile, Irène reflected, she had accepted his plan in outline. She was in Crete, accompanied by a young woman of unremarkable appearance only some seven years older than Tammam. They were members of a package tour organized from London, and would be herded through on the return journey without question, changing at Athens for Brussels, with barely a glance at the passport photographs. When Irène went home her newly recovered daughter would be on the same plane—not too close to seem to have any connection, but where Irène could keep an eye on her, cover up if anything went wrong. She would have to look a little different from how Zeid described her, but not enough like Sylvie for any of the Fiesta crowd to see she was taking her place. As for Sylvie herself, it was unfortunate, but she must suffer some slight mishap that required her to catch a later flight. And sometime just before her expected departure there would be a robbery in the hotel. Hers would be among the passports and currency taken.

It would take some careful organizing. Irène could foresee the complicated parts of her own role, notably at the airport in claiming the boarding cards for them both from the Fiesta agent.

What frightened her more, although she refused to look directly at the possibilities, was how Zeid intended to delay Sylvie Audoin's departure from Crete long enough to ensure that Tammam was clear of the second leg of her journey and safely in Brussels. Sylvie was a simple-minded romantic but there was no call to injure her. As Zeid was a fanatic and this was a venture very close to his heart, there was no way of being utterly sure that he wouldn't . . . wouldn't overlook considerations of everyone's wellbeing.

Irène lay in the sun mellowing the copper tan which complimented the taut, disciplined lines of her body, and her mind ranged over a number of possibilities whereby she might pre-empt any move by her ex-husband and handle the homecoming part of the plan herself.

Paula returned from Fódele with a string bag full of oranges, the gift of a farmer whom she'd met on the bus going there. He had been determined to practise his atrocious English and clapped his hands joyfully over her few phrases of Greek. Once there, he had personally conducted her round the village, introducing her generously, and proudly told her his own garbled version of the El Greco story.

She had been pressed to stay on and take an early evening

meal of slow-stewed lamb, peppers, honey cakes, fruit and wine with his womenfolk in the cool farmhouse, and they had all turned out to put her on the bus back to Iraklion. Warm, earthy, utterly normal, as was the village too. She had looked in vain here for the tremulous distortions of El Greco's paintings.

Arrived back at the hotel, she went straight up to the card lounge to unload her bounty. Fresh oranges with their green twigs and leaves on them were still novelty enough to delight tourists however blasé they had grown over five thousand years of buried civilization.

Everyone from Fiesta seemed to be there, either playing bridge or watching. 'Sweetie, I wish you'd look out for Des,' his mother said, frowning over her cards and sniffing appreciatively at her orange. 'He's in a very awkward mood. That wretched Kápetan's been at him again, asking questions. Now Des says he didn't see anyone at all on the roof. It's not like him to tell lies.'

'I don't see what I can do about it.'

'Jolly him up a little. He likes you. He's dreadfully in the dumps.'

'Solve the mystery with your legalistic mind,' suggested Foden sardonically, partnering Mrs Van Leiden.

Paula sat down, still in earshot of their table. Behind her she could hear Frau Toller talking with the nurses and Jozsef's occasional quiet bids. Farther on, two of the Canadian Widows were squawking over the poor hands dealt them by Malcolm Bowles, while Miss Pallett smirked at hers.

Malcolm Bowles, Paula thought. He was the one who'd heard her tell Melissa she studied Law. Foden hadn't been there at the time. The little snippet of information had probably been general currency round the tables during play. So, they gossiped about her when she wasn't there. Not surprising, perhaps, in their idle moments. They were at it even now, following up Mrs Van Leiden's reference to

Des's questioning. The subject of their speculation and innuendo was the young Egyptian beauty who'd been making the vanity film. Surely the police couldn't seriously believe she'd any connection with her own little brother's death? And wasn't it to be expected that she'd deny being unaccompanied in the roof garden with her Arab admirer at such an hour, when normally so jealously chaperoned?

Paula pictured the scene, a breeze gently moving the fronds of palms and oleanders in their tubs; moonlight laying a silver trellis over the darker pool; stars in the indigo sky, street lamps and windows brightening the darkness below. Warm, aromatic, romantic. Dangerous.

If Des had been there without their seeing him, couldn't the boy Sayid have been equally hidden in the shadows? Watching. Listening. He was an Arab and also spoke some French. He would have understood what they said.

That would be what the police Kápetan wanted to be sure about—whether the girl, or more likely the man, had any special reason to fear being overheard.

She looked up and saw Foden's eyes on her meaningfully. He'd worked it out and waited for her to reach the same point. With half an ear she was aware of the voices continuing round her, sharp with one-upmanship. While the bridge-players pondered a mean hand their tongues scored independently. The psychic climate sparked with animus. Rashly the RAF moustache's overweight sister attempted to upstage Mrs Van Leiden with a mention of their yacht at Bridport. That buoyant lady took her time consulting her hand, then promptly sank her with a query about displacement and rigging. The brother trod water briefly, admitting they 'only hired the old tub. Must say I'm more of a dry bob myself.'

'C'mon, *Marjorie!*' the Torontan Kate rallied her partner loudly. Mildred—Miriam? Muriel?—Pallett bridled. Bowles tittered. Kate knew exactly what she'd done. She winked across at Paula. 'Tangerine, if you meet the bar waiter on your way, hasten him, will you? Some of us need reviving.'

The closer they grew, the more they were approaching the unstoppered malice of a group-therapy session. Package tour or psychiatric unit? Paula asked herself; but in any case she would not stay on for any inquest on their play, which at this rate threatened to be lethal. As she reached the door Mrs Van Leiden called again without lifting her eyes from her cards, 'He's probably down at the fruit machines.'

Paula halted. '*Star Wars*,' she corrected. Was Mrs Van L deliberately lagging a generation in the rear?

'Whatever. He cleared me out of drachmas, then made off.'

'Drunk on wine gums by now, I shouldn't wonder,' Paula mocked. 'No promises, but if I do chance to see him . . .' She nodded.

'Bless you for a sweetie. Perilous job being a mum. Be warned and get yourself some early practice.'

Even although she knew Des's mother was genuinely concerned, her apparent levity left a sour taste. Paula looked back at her uninterrupted play. At the next table all movement was arrested. Frau Toller had frozen in disapproval, a card held face down in the air. Irène Petitjean darted a venomous glare across at Mrs Van Leiden. Jozsef sat bowed between the two, smiling gently. 'Two clubs, I think,' he murmured in French.

Paula left them at their cards. Downstairs Des was no-where to be seen; the bar waiter was already overloaded with orders. She shrugged off her commissions and went out to the warm, scented Greek night.

Daytime traffic had dwindled. Everyone seemed to be afoot, making—she discovered—for the harbour and its old Venetian fortress. She let the flow carry her along. At the apparent rallying point there were blue-painted benches arranged, with a band of some dozen self-consciously proud musicians in baggy white tunics waiting to begin. Almost instantly a small, wiry man ran up and stood before the group, clapped for silence, stood on tiptoe and raised his hands.

There was something raw about the sound. It had the keening of a bagpipe and the rhythmic thump of mediæval music. As soon as the conductor had them going he was in there himself with a flared reed pipe, wildly soaring above the others, ever urging them on to a more abandoned tempo. Abruptly the air ended as if broken off, and an unaccompanied male voice, strident and barbaric, rose over the ensemble of *bouzouki*, lute, tambourine and fiddles, growing wilder and faster with each chorus until the crowd was stamping and swaying, humming tight-lipped.

And then the dancing began, first with three women in the old, country costume of long, embroidered skirt, wide-sleeved blouse and bright kerchief, moving in the fluid figures with abrupt, silent pauses when they froze like statues. After this, wilder music and the crowd breaking up to dance in circles. Paula found herself pulled in, linked up, stamping and swaying, drooping, twirling and trotting as the others moved on either side.

Breathless at last, she reached a terrace café and broke free. At her table two of the musicians joined her, one young, giraffe-like and bespectacled, the other old, in gleaming knee-high boots and baggy black trousers. He wore a kind of gipsy cap and had a ferocious smile crowded with long, yellow teeth. In Greek he told Paula she was paler than the moon, wise as Athina, delicious as honey. All just within her guessing-vocabulary. She replied that he was as kind as he was handsome, and he roared with amusement. 'You *understand*, English lady? You speak some Greek? Wonderful!'

So then she had to dance with him, and as they found their seats again Paula passed the ex-schoolmistress Ella Sharp with Ben Kimber complacently in tow. She was earnestly explaining these were Klephts, once guerrilla bandits in the north mainland, but now professional gipsy musicians. Paula's glass was refilled with *retsina*. Extravagant toasts were being drunk, first to Hellas, then to her people, her visitors, to any name at all called out from the grinning faces around. Paula thought she even heard 'Danny Kaye' and 'Lord Byron'. These Greeks had long memories.

A space was clearing, half-illumined, with shadowed areas around. From these slowly emerged strange, lean creatures with cropped hair and whitened faces, garishly painted with patterns which continued down bare chests and arms. They wore only what looked like frayed jeans which clung to their emaciated legs.

There were five of them in all, probably males, but one seldom saw more than any two at a time, often just a solo dancer. All their movements were in total silence, a sort of melancholy, symbolistic mime which no one seemed quite to understand or like. After the riot of loud music it was eerie in the extreme. Sinister, and it disturbed her.

One of the Klephts rose from his table shaking a fist and shouted a word. The women near him *shushed* and turned away their heads.

'What did he say?' Paula asked.

The old man was reluctant. 'I don't know the English. It is when one goes bad, generation after generation. Something like that.'

'Decadent? Degenerates?'

'Perhaps. But he should not say it aloud. They are foreigners, and different. We in Greece wish to be friends with all.'

Even gipsies, it seemed, repeated the propaganda formulas.

'What kind of foreigners?'

'From Northern Europe. Sweden, Germany, Denmark sometimes. And Britain. They meet here, live in their own way. Die young.'

As silently as they'd come and as they'd danced and

been watched, the mimers disappeared. She supposed that somehow their performance would be rewarded, but no one was collecting money. They frightened her, seeming less than human but more vulnerable. Perhaps already more injured.

'It is mainly on Kríti that you find them,' the old gipsy explained. 'Not here in Iraklion, but at Mátala on the south coast there used to be many, many. They lived in the caves but the police drove them out, to villages. They are like the mad prophets of the old days.'

Lost children of the north, Paula thought. Dropouts, hopheads, junkies, mental descendants of the Flower People of the 'sixties. And even the gipsies condemned them. Suddenly she found the sadness unbearable. She rose to go, and hands reached out to force her back. '*Efkharistó polí*,' she told them all. 'Thank you so much, but I must go now.'

'Back to your husband; good, good,' said the old man and he held up one hand like a blessing. But Paula had been friends long enough with Dímitra to know Greek ways. She planted a kiss on each of his leathery cheeks, shaking both his hands, and then was passed round his whole group for the same. She knew that behind her they would go on singing and dancing until daylight. It was the warmest and wildest evening she could remember. These spontaneous people had reached right through her. Nothing was left of her native reserve or caution.

Until she was half way back to the hotel, in the now hushed and more deserted streets uptown.

Then she was quite certain that someone was following, some fifty feet behind, slipping from doorway to doorway, halting as she halted. Someone large and lumbering, yet who could stay silent and fade into the shadows when she turned to look back.

Paula walked faster, then began to run.

CHAPTER 10

Still he was hanging on. She ran left, turned right and left again to come out on the same route, hoping to throw him off her tracks, but when she reached 25th August Street he reappeared, the same distance behind. With fear hammering in her throat she reminded herself of Andy Whitelaw's words, 'We have no crime on Crete.'

Of course not. They made it look like accident, to keep the records clean. Little boys fell off roofs, weren't pushed. An accident could happen to her, though she couldn't see why it should have to.

Breathless, she burst into Eleftherías Square where at last there were plenty of people and lights almost as bright as day. She slowed to a long stride and made for the hotel, pushed through the glass doors and fell into a chair that faced out. Now she would clearly see who came in next. Here, in the foyer, she was safe, but from whom, and for how long?

It unnerved her that she couldn't guess at the man's identity any more than at his intention. It could have been any mugger, a stranger picking on her as an unknown, but it didn't feel like that. There had been a sense of purpose in the following. She had passed through groups of walkers, doubled back, run part of the way, and he hadn't been shaken off. *He knew she was aware of him*, and he still came on, inexorably. She shut her eyes a moment. It had been someone she knew; a large, lumbering man. Few island Greeks were so big.

Andy Whitelaw was heavily built, clumsy-seeming. It could have been him, if he indulged in a secret Jekyll-and-Hyde existence. Unlikely. Fiesta arrangements kept him too busy. Yet she felt she knew whoever it had been. Who else fitted into the description?

The phoney RAF moustache had the right build. He was a patter and petter when he got the chance, but she couldn't see such persistence in him. She doubted if he could manage much more than a suggestive leer. The sight of a Metaxa brandy bottle en route would certainly divert him from any sexual intentions. He'd looked pretty laid back at cards a couple of hours ago. His next port of call should have been bed.

The Colonel had a large frame, although fleshless. But he moved quite differently, with a disciplined stiffness. The follower had seemed to lurch, yet was lithe enough to slide into shadow when she turned to confront him. Heavy. Muscled, not fat. No, certainly not Colonel Martin, who was doubtless as kind and decent as he always seemed.

Who else? Ben Kimber was quite small for a man, and Ella was in charge tonight. Malcolm Bowles was small too. One of the disturbing things about Bowles, she now realized, was that he had the head of a large man, a Roman with authority, but it was set on a miniature body. That, and the curiously silver eyes, was what made her uneasy. But it hadn't been Bowles following her tonight with such intent, even if—as Mrs Van L had said—his looks at Paula could have killed.

There was surely someone else heavily built as well as Andy, Colonel Martin and The Moustache. Someone who'd given that impression of towering over her. It had been when she sat here in the hotel. Someone coming towards her, carrying—

Yes, the bearlike man who put in odd hours in the Maze Bar. The barman who'd somehow known she had gone to Knossos on the local bus.

And then, while the image of that man was still in her mind, another appeared, and he was more scaring still. That was the senior policeman who had questioned her after

Sayid's fall. The one Mrs Van L had called the Kápetan.

She became aware that she was being stared at from Reception. It was the androgynous Cretan who'd been with Bowles at Knossos. She looked coolly at him, the man who had spoiled for her the Prince of Lilies fresco. It was true he had similar features, the same graceful slightness of body, but she found herself frowning. He simpered back.

There was quite a pause before the swing doors opened and two people came in together, tensely at odds. Des made straight for her. '*There* you are,' he declared, red-faced. 'Are you all right? You know he was following you?'

Jozsef looked more distressed than guilty. 'Sit down,' Paula commanded drily. 'You must be out of breath. I was.'

He slid into the next chair and for a moment hid his face in his hands, then he looked up. 'The boy is right, I was behind you a lot of the way. But it was the man I was following, the one who was so interested in you. We saw him from our window. My mother will tell you if you wish to phone and ask. You walked by on the far side of the road and he came after you, furtively, trying not to be noticed. We were afraid he meant some kind of mischief. I didn't expect to come so fast, or so far.'

'I'm sorry, that was my fault,' Paula said, 'because I ran. I will phone your mother, but to tell her you've arrived safely. And I'll see you are brought something to drink. What would you prefer?' She stood up to go for attendance, but the little assistant manager was there with his hesitant smile. 'Is something wrong? Can I help you?'

On an impulse Paula gave him a brief idea of what had happened. He wrung his hands a little and made sympathetic noises. 'I know there's no crime on Crete,' Paula said grimly. 'But I didn't like it.'

He brought a telephone across and plugged it in by their chairs, then he sent a boy for coffee. Jozsef was able to speak to his mother and assure her that nothing alarming had occurred. He would order a taxi for his return. 'Go to bed now, Mother,' he told her in German. 'Good night.'

'So you didn't see who it was?' Paula asked Des, pouring the coffee from a ceramic jug.

'I saw *him*,' Des insisted, glowering at Jozsef. 'Well, there might have been someone else too. He wasn't always just where I expected.' He frowned at the Austrian. 'And sometimes you looked—*he* looked—sort of bulky. But it was you in the Square.'

'Jozsef,' Paula asked, 'did you see him clearly at all?'

He nodded. 'Once I caught sight of him under a lamp. I would know him again. But he was a stranger to me.'

'Would he be a local or a visitor?'

'Impossible to say. But not any visitor here at this hotel. We have had so many meals here that I would have seen him before. I am afraid that's not much help.'

Des stayed with her while she saw Jozsef into his taxi, thanking him for his kind concern. 'You too, Des,' she said as they went back indoors. 'I'm grateful for the knight errant stuff.'

'Any time,' he said grandly. 'Hey, you had a good time down at the harbour with those gipsies. I saw you there first.'

'Didn't I just! I wasn't expecting all that music. I went down thinking I might run into you.'

Des's jaw jutted. 'Not more questions. I'm not saying any more—'

'I can't blame you. It's hell when no one believes the truth. But it's not Sayid I'm interested in so much as the Kápetan.'

The boy cocked a supercilious eyebrow. 'Gipsies and the Fuzz. You're kinky, you know.'

'Listen, Des. Before you came in, dragging poor Jozsef, I was thinking of all the big, hulking men it could have been. And they all belong here at the hotel. Jozsef has seen them. But he never saw the Kápetan, because

Jozsef didn't have to make a statement. He wasn't here overnight.'

'But why should a policeman want to follow you?' Des demanded, bewildered. 'I mean, why *professionally*?'

Paula looked amused. 'That was almost a compliment, Des.'

'Accidents happen,' he admitted. 'Like on the roof.'

'How much *didn't* the police believe, then?'

'That I saw anyone up there. Those two arguing, I mean. They wanted me to say I was with that boy Sayid and we were chucking a quoit about. That's what would fit in with everyone else's statement.'

'So the girl denied being there, and the man backed her up?'

'The police seemed to think she might have lied if it suited her, but the man had three friends who gave him an alibi. They said he was with them in Rethymnon at midnight. Well, obviously the police accepted that and threw out my story. So I changed it to suit everyone. And that's how it stands.'

'What about the quoit? And Sayid?'

'Nothing to do with me. Somebody else did all the chucking.'

'Des, how were you so sure *who* it was up there? It's pretty inky in places, and I don't suppose they were keen to be seen.'

'At first I didn't know who they were, but when he got quite mad he started swearing. They were the only words I know in Arabic. I learnt them last year when we went to Tangier. And then when the girl got up to go she walked past the floodlight and I saw right through her clothes. Those Turkish trousers.'

'Harem pants? Yes, I remember she was wearing them. So she lied. They both lied.'

'I know that, and you know that, but who's going to believe us? Not the Kápetan.'

'So what's he up to? Why pick on me to follow? He knows I was down at ground level when it happened, whatever happened.'

Des grinned impishly. 'Same as the gipsies, maybe. Took a fancy to you. There's no accounting for tastes!'

Next morning when Paula gave up her key at Reception she was handed her post, which had come by last night's flight. There was a viewcard of Jersey from her mother, hoping that she was enjoying herself, and a three-page scrawl from Angus with details for their sailing holiday He would meet her at Heathrow and she could put up at his flat for the night, ready for an early start next day for Chichester harbour. Just over three days ahead now, Paula reckoned, and then she'd see Angus again. It was another world, and one she was eager for. Separation had made her feelings clearer, crystallized her view of him. Now she was quite certain that he was the-man-likeliest.

There was mail for Irène Petitjean too, delivered by messenger. Her hand, as she took the square yellow envelope, trembled a little. Zeid had addressed it correctly, using the maiden name she'd reverted to. Not like the messenger who'd sought her out last autumn in Brussels, asking her flatmate for 'Madame Khalida'. She had had to deny all knowledge of the name, then managed to trace the man later and show him proof of her previous identity. Zeid was a fool to imagine that once they'd parted so bitterly and he'd kidnapped their tiny daughter she would be proud to admit she'd married a PLO man. Now even he saw the wisdom of the change, disillusioned with the cruel regime he'd been working for. She had a safe, long-established niche in respectable society, totally unconnected with his past. If he had covered his own movements equally carefully there was no reason why Tammam should ever be traced to Belgium. Just to be doubly sure, however, both women would have to live separate lives, with a new identity tailored for the girl, and here Irène found herself dangerously short of information on Tammam's background and abilities. She would make a poor student nurse if all her training consisted of assembling and firing a Kalashnikov automatic rifle.

But this letter should contain a lot of what she needed to know, also the detailed plan for Tammam's reception and —most exciting of all—her photograph.

Irène hid the envelope in her magazine and went up to her room to collect her swimsuit for a dip in the roof pool. She could be relatively private there. Sylvie complained perpetually of their hotel being in town instead of by the sea, but she seldom went up for a swim, preferring to lounge on their balcony, reading her romantic trash and turning raspberry red unobserved. She seemed to have been scared off her reason for coming here, which made small difference to Irène, although she despised the girl for letting inertia take over where before she had at least some kind of aim in life. As far as Irène was concerned, she had served her purpose in providing a credible reason for their coming here together. Sylvie might sulk or have second thoughts as she pleased. It made no difference to Irène whether she found herself a husband or not. All that mattered now was that when they were due to travel home, in ten days' time, she should be stricken by some sudden, last-minute illness that made her unfit to go. Meanwhile Irène was free to pursue her holiday interests and plan how best to effect Tammam's safe departure.

Stretched on her towel on the pool's terrace, Irène opened her letter and the photograph fell out.

But Tammam was beautiful!—quite startlingly so, very dark with enormous eyes and perfect bones. An Arab, with the early maturity of eastern women, she had her father's high-bridged nose and straight mouth. But *my frame*, Irene acknowledged, looking long. This one will be a handful to manage. She will want to do everything *her* way, even when she has no experience of the things to be done. And then

Irène smiled, because her daughter had to be like that. She'd been awkward enough herself, defied the world to follow her own will. Until she learned better. The hard way.

She slipped the photograph into her beachbag and opened out the letter. It was handwritten in French, with many underlinings. She frowned, running through it quickly. There had been a change of plan. They must get Tammam away at once. The exodus was brought forward by a week.

Zeid would bring her, before Tuesday daybreak, by *caïque*, but would not himself be landing. His absence from Tobruk would be remarked on for any longer period. The address to which Tammam would be taken was within an hour's drive of Mátala, and would be notified to Irène not more than four hours before her arrival. It was essential that she be picked up immediately and removed to a place of safety in utmost secrecy until part two of the escape could be effected as formerly planned. By this he obviously meant departure from Iraklion airport to Athens using the Fiesta booking of Sylvie Audoin.

Impossible, Irène decided. How could Tammam be kept hidden for a whole week in a place where she, Irène, was a complete stranger? No hotel vacancies existed in mid-season. If she started making inquiries it would be a secret no longer. Everyone would wonder who was the extra person she was accommodating. Damn Zeid to hell for an incompetent fool, too concerned wth his own safety to take adequate precautions himself on the other side! If Tammam had to be kept so carefully hidden it meant that someone was after her. Irène would herself be drawing the fire off Zeid. Could he have intended that, the vindictive savage that he was, because long ago she had refused to submit to unendurable servitude? Did he want her eliminated?

No, because this was all about Tammam, and he wanted her protected. However ruthless he'd become he still felt the love of a father for his child. The letter spoke only too clearly of his anxiety for her. Of near-panic.

She went through it again. Basically the original plan still held. The change was in the timing: a week less to plan in; a week extra to cover up Tammam's presence. There had to be some alternative way to tackle it. If only it somehow could become necessary for Irène and Sylvie to go home early, cutting the holiday in half. Then they would have to take the place of others due to return this next Wednesday.

No, it wasn't even necessary to have two places. One would be enough, for Tammam herself, if she was capable of travelling alone. The main thing was to get her on her way, confuse the pursuit. And if, through Zeid's stupidity or malice, the trail should lead to Irène, wasn't it better that she should be openly here as scheduled, unaware of any irregularities?

Who was supposed to be leaving this Wednesday? The six Canadian women certainly, returning via London. And the English girl Paula.

Paula had dark hair too, but long on her shoulders. Tammam's was short and curly, cropped like a boy soldier's. But with a wig and paler make-up, wouldn't she get by quite well with the English girl's passport photograph? They were more alike than Tammam and Sylvie, and certainly closer in age. Why shouldn't she modify the plan herself and clear Tammam through a week in advance?

Think! she commanded herself. If she goes as the Paula girl she needs her papers, her luggage. When she gets to Athens, what happens? She's supposed to change aircraft and go on all the way to London. Another four and a half or five hours when someone might challenge her identity in front of people who knew the real Paula. Horribly risky, but if it came off and Tammam reached London, Irène had friends there, ex-patients, of whom she could ask a favour. They would give the girl a room, take care of her until Irène could get back and make some more permanent arrangement.

It would be ideal, because no one could possibly suspect

a link between Zeid and London. This was a far better plan than replacing Sylvie, because now that little numbskull could return normally with Irène who would be free of all suspicion. It would be Paula who stayed behind, in hospital, ꞌnaware that her passport had been stolen and her luggage sent ahead.

But again the difficulty lay in the timing. It was better for Paula to be incapacitated *for at least a week*, while Irène completed her second half of the Cretan holiday. Something more serious than she'd had in mind for Sylvie. And to happen at the very last moment, so that no one heard of it before the plane left. Even, if necessary, something permanent, so that Paula never had a chance to voice suspicions about who it was working against her!

There was a terrible lot here for Irène to undertake on her own, now that Zeid wasn't coming ashore. But he had given her the name of a fisherman at Mátala. Damon Skoufas. He would do anything, Zeid said, and stay silent forever, if you paid him enough. And, as an extra precaution, she had brought in her luggage some little extras from the drug cupboard. Being a hospital Sister had its uses.

She groaned under her breath, and the next sunbather looked up curiously. This was no place to mastermind such a complicated campaign. She needed to be totally alone and get down to it with paper and a pen. It would have to be put off for the present, because after lunch she and Sylvie were due to go with Frau Toller and Jozsef by car to view the Plain of Lassithi with its thousands of windmills. Wasting the best part of a day, when in forty-eight hours she needed to have the whole operation planned in detail and foolproofed. On the other hand it was essential to behave in a normal manner, as a visitor enchanted with the island and having no slightest care to distract her from sun and socializing and sightseeing.

CHAPTER 11

Des reported shortly that Mom had had enough. She had decided on the instant that she needed a more sophisticated setting than Crete. They were off to Athens tonight, by ferry boat because there were no vacancies by air.

'It's the Sayid thing, isn't it?' Paula asked.

'She thinks that if one boy "falls off the roof", another will.'

'Well, you did notice more than anyone else, about the time that it happened. If you've gone away the case is obviously closed. She has a point.'

'But I like Crete. There's so much I haven't seen yet. And it's got *Knossos*!' His voice was agonized, belying the basilisk face.

Paula made up her mind quickly. 'Let's go and see it again, right now. We'll take a picnic. Wear your emerald T-shirt, Des. Expand a bit.'

'*Morituri*,' he pronounced lugubriously, '*te salutamus*.'

Paula snorted. 'Fine, if you like to think of it that way. But go out with panache.'

'Our own personal earthquake.' He was beginning to enjoy his martyr's role. Then suddenly, 'What sort of picnic?'

'Look, go tell your mother where we're off to, while I fetch a haversack. Then we'll shop our way down to the bus stop. They probably have anti-litter laws about not eating at the Palace site, but there are some lovely places farther on down the valley.'

'I've never been that far.'

'All the more reason to go. But make sure your mother knows.'

They met up in the foyer and Des had come alive again.

Down by the Lion Fountain they bought fresh-baked fruity bread, white goat's cheese, apricots, figs, honey cakes and unresinated wine. 'We can get kebabs and Turkish coffee at a taverna nearby,' Paula promised.

They bounced off in the local bus and were made welcome with the usual pantomime of exaggerated smiles and gestures from the Cretan locals.

It was Des's turn to lead the way round the ruins once they had firmly refused the persistent guides. He organized the route systematically, marching straight to the North Entrance of the excavation, then covering every stairway, passage and court until the East and West Wings. After about twenty minutes of silent following, Paula sat on the hot, sandy rock, her back against a wild almond tree, and stared at the shaded fresco of the bull. When at last she went to find him Des was standing motionless before the great Sacred Horns, gazing through at the skyline framed between. 'That's Mount Jouktas,' he said as Paula came up behind. 'The Holy Mountain.'

'Yes. The neolithic people used to make human sacrifice up there,' Paula told him. 'Quite a lot of remains have been dug up.'

'Do you think that's what happened to the youths and maidens sent over from the mainland as tribute?'

'Possibly. But I prefer to think they came to train as acrobats for the bull dances you see on friezes and the sides of vases. Maybe they didn't actually disappear but just stayed on here, grew older and married, had children, forgot Athens and died in the natural course of things.'

'But Mount Jouktas might have wanted them. To be appeased, so that it wouldn't make any more earthquakes.' Des had his brooding look back. He shook his head at the distant horizon and turned away. Then he went back to pacing, moodily kicking at stones, padding in and out of the labyrinthine passages and chambers. When he came back, his agitation worked off, he scowled at her, hands deep in pockets. 'She ought to marry again, don't you think? Why doesn't she?'

It was his mother who worried him, she saw. Paula shook her head to show she wasn't getting involved.

'Did yours?'

'My mother? Repeatedly.' Her voice was dry. 'It never turned out as she hoped, though.'

'Does it ever?' He sounded baffled, really wanting to know.

Paula struggled to be fair. 'I think the first time must always have the best chance of success. Whatever success is.'

'Mom's awful the way she is. But she'd be worse if she— you know—kept marrying again.' He looked at her appraisingly. 'Will you get married?'

'I haven't given it a lot of thought. Been too busy with my work, taking exams and so on. But at the back of my mind I must have assumed that one day I would. In general terms. Then, lately—'

'You have a lover,' he declared flatly.

'No. I have a good friend who happens to be a man. He's someone I'd enjoy being with over a long period. At least, I think so. We're going sailing together when I get back.'

'You may find you can't stand him after all.'

'Could be. Crewing is quite a test. In that case it's no go. And, of course, he may discover the same about me.'

Des scoffed. He shuffled off again. 'I'm going round once more, just a flash. See you at the exit?'

She watched him trudge off, tough and vulnerable, just a bit of a braggart in his uncertainty, cagily hurt, and at present intent on squeezing its utmost essence out of Knossos, like a sucked orange.

She looked around and recognized a shift of possession about the place. When she first came Knossos had been her father's. Today it belonged to Des wretchedly saying goodbye. She would come once more before she left Crete, and then it would be her own.

She tried to explain this to Foden when she sat with him that evening in Eleftherías Square. He was in his brief stage between dour sobriety and sardonic inebriety when he seemed actually to listen. She found herself explaining her childhood wonder, the shared obsession when instead of fairy tales her father re-created for her the legends of Homer. Icarus, Minos, Pasiphae, Theseus and Ariadne had taken the place of Red Ridinghood and Cinderella in her infant mind. Bull-leaping athletes and bare-breasted snake goddesses had filled the picture-books given her by that gentle, loving man who had quietly died in his armchair one November night when she was ten and her mother out at one of her charity concerts.

She had thought that Foden was getting glazed with *ouzo*, but he had watched her as if through a moving mist, and when she fell silent he began to talk of his son.

It was all in the past tense, told without sequence so that although she knew at once that the boy was dead she had to listen carefully and try the jigsaw pieces together before they'd fit. A story of guilt, of self-absorbed contentment with marriage, family and career, abruptly ruptured at his wife's death in a car crash; and the chill realization that nothing was as he'd assumed. The cool, detached young man under his roof was an enigmatic stranger with alien values, who condemned his father's planned passage and chose to drift rudderless, living through his senses.

'When you're young,' Foden said bleakly, 'it matters so much how the external world gets to you; its music, its language, the clothes you must display yourself in, what you eat or leave uneaten. Sensation is everything; duty and habit merely serve to obscure it. Grow older and you know that the only real thing is what you're dragging round inside you. A void, an ache, a chill. Briefly, if you're lucky, a faint glow. But that is all there is, and you know that's what you've become. And that is what Hell is.'

Paula sat staring down at her clenched hands. But what had happened to the boy? How old had he been when he died? And why? Foden didn't say this and she dared not ask him. Somewhere there had been a parallel with her own experience, which had made the man talk, just as hers had been in parallel with Des's, and Des's with the grown-up but dependent Jozsef's. The parent-child thing—the most intimate, guilt-ridden relationship she had ever tried to understand. Tried and failed.

She left Foden before he could reach the sharp, coruscating level of his evening bridge sessions when his blood alcohol allowed him back into the social rat-race. She was ashamed that she knew no way to help him, suffering as he did now. When he reached the bitterly witty stage she could never connect with him, and sober he was all reinforced carapace, the feeling parts pulled inside. Between the two it must be—as he'd said—Hell, to be himself.

She saw the Van Leidens briefly before they left the hotel. Des was unfamiliar in a blue denim suit, his tously hair slicked straight with water. His mother—improbably, for the ferry boat—wore a Leghorn straw hat and matching two-piece in cream silk shantung. Yet not so silly, Paula reflected. Dressed like that she'd be assured of jet-set treatment wherever she went. There would be a respectful space all round, like germs kept at bay by an antibiotic presence.

Paula shook hands solemnly with Des and had her cheek lightly brushed by his mother's. She handed the boy a slip of paper. 'My phone number, in case you're ever on the loose in London.'

'Forward hussy,' Mrs Van L said mildly. ''Bye, sweetie. I wish you were coming with us. No chance of a quick visit between planes on Wednesday?'

'I'm afraid not. It's too tight a timetable. Have a wonderful time. Don't miss going to Epidavros, Des. Look, there's your taxi.'

Des went out to it doggedly, not looking back, like the sub-hero of a rebel film heading in the final reel for the firing-squad. For all that she was aware of something comic in his melodrama, Paula was saddened too. This sense of loss and the level of sympathy she'd felt for parents like Mrs Van L and Foden made her more ready now to allow the Frau Dok's attempt to monopolize her last day. Not that there was any reason to resist the kindly offered invitation. It had been tentatively mentioned before, after the incident with Jozsef in the lift: a day's outing by hire car to the southern coast of Crete, taking in the Roman ruins of Gortyn, Minoan Phaestos, and the neolithic caves overhanging the bay of Mátala. It was a unique opportunity, beyond what her restricted funds allowed, and they were interesting company, the Frau Doktor perhaps a little formidable, but Jozsef's gentleness more than compensating.

Frau Toller had been hovering while the Van Leidens took their leave, and she buttonholed Paula as the girl turned away. 'The day after tomorrow, then?' she instructed. 'The car will pick you up here at a quarter to nine. Bring your swimsuit and suntan cream, but no food. We are taking all the food and drink we shall need for the day, in an icebox.'

'You're very kind, Frau Toller.'

'Magda, please.' Unexpectedly the old lady inclined her iron-grey head and kissed Paula's cheek. Then she nodded briskly, caught Jozsef's eye across the foyer and went out with him into the sunshine.

So that had disposed of the age-old mind-teaser: how to make use of a holiday's last day. As a schoolgirl Paula had agonized over her own indecision, torn between so many desires that couldn't be fulfilled again for at least two months. In the end she had often spoilt the precious time with her own dissatisfaction, but next day she would always wake up calmly ready for whatever came.

Monday was for clearing up odd jobs, finishing her shopping. Now she must find two extra gifts, for Jozsef and his mother, as a way of saying thank-you. She already had half a dozen purchases ready labelled but unwrapped because of eventually going through the Customs. There was an embroidered blouse for her flatmate Lottie, a çeramic dish for Nan Yeadings, handmade leather belts for all the men except Angus. For him she had bought what must surely be the most enormous bath sponge fished from the southern Med that summer. She had smiled at the Freudian implications, admitting that Angus certainly would look good at the other end of it.

She set out her purchases on the little round table of her balcony and sat soaking in the sunshine. Across the small square below, empty but for a delivery van and a clump of palm trees leaning over a circular wall, she saw a sudden glint in an opposite window. It was a more modern building prosaically constructed of concrete. Various pictorial signs and slogans advertised the offices which spread over three floors above the street-level shops.

The building backed on to the light. What she saw could have been glinting sunlight only if it had struck her hotel first and then been reflected in some glassy surface. Suddenly it was repeated, a white light flashing from behind slanted venetian blinds, as though a camera was being used between their louvres.

As she watched, the blind was raised at one end of the window and someone stood there, a dumpy white cruciform, hands to face so that the arms appeared truncated. The flesh of them looked very dark against the white of the shirt.

The figure stood up straight—he must be quite six feet tall—and moved away from the camera which stayed supported on a tripod invisible to her.

This side of her hotel was washed with brilliant light like a stage. Paula looked back and saw that the bedroom, as well as the balcony, must be clearly visible from across the square. And so too were all the rooms which faced this way. It was impossible to tell which it was that the snooper was concentrated on.

On an impulse Paula reached down by her feet for her own camera, guessed distance, exposure, speed, and shot off two frames to finish the spool, focusing squarely on the observer's window.

There, the spy espied! Not perhaps that there was necessarily anything sinister in what he did. There could be a dozen reasons for a camera buff acting so, and doubtless there were many degrees of voyeurism, from casual curiosity about the globe-trotting 'other half' to the more deadly prying with intent. She reminded herself drily that there was no crime on Crete. But things happened. Only two nights back she had been followed persistently in the street and been frightened. And there had been little Sayid's 'accident'. Could this man have any connection with either occurrence? Even perhaps be from the police, keeping an eye on what happened over here?

She stood up and started gathering her things together, but stopped to stare across at the window opposite. The man was caught bending forward, intent on her movements. He reached back for a jacket and started pulling it on. The venetian blind came down again, the slats half closed.

Paula felt a pulse beating in her throat. It was ridiculous to be afraid. She was quite safe here. Even if he could still watch her through the louvres and with some telescopic device, she had only to draw her curtains. Then she could leave the hotel from the opposite side before he reached it.

But out there he would still be able to recognize her, while she had no way of knowing who he was.

Do what, then? Stay here behind the curtains for half an hour until the coast seemed clear? Then go out dressed differently and wearing dark glasses? No, that was out of all proportion. Just because a man peeped once, it didn't mean he'd devote his life to it, for the same female. Carry on normally then, only stay alert. No curtains, no disguise, go shopping as planned, take the exposed film to the 24-hour service shop in 25th August Street. Buy something nice for the Frau Dok and her son. Nothing was going to happen. Tonight she'd tell Foden about it and they'd both laugh at her needless alarm. Tomorrow she'd be away all day with Magda and Jozsef, and the next day—home to Angus.

She got rid of the film first, then toured the curio shops until she found an unusual little bronze Herakles, elongated like a Quixote, nude but topped with a Grecian helmet, and with the fleshless wishbone legs she normally associated with Etruscan figures. It cost more than she'd intended but would serve both recipients, a touristic piece of *kitsch* to remind them of Iraklion. For herself she'd bought nothing. The memories, she thought, would be lasting enough.

It was half way down to the harbour that Paula felt herself being watched, but when she looked round it was only the older of the two Belgian nurses standing in the doorway of a hairdressing salon and staring fixedly after her. When Paula lifted a hand in greeting it seemed to disconcert her. She had already stepped back as if to hide, but then she changed her mind, grimaced and waved back. She appeared to be alone, and Paula wondered where Sylvie Audoin was. The younger nurse didn't go many places on her own.

In Makarios Street, near the Historical Museum, a bus for Rethymnon and Chania was just about to leave. At roughly three drax per kilometre Paula guessed she could afford it and ran to get on. Beaches of golden sand beckoned her, and her bikini was at the bottom of her tote bag.

Because there were a lot of holiday sites on this side of Iraklion the busbound locals were correspondingly more blasé. They contented themselves with playing up a little to the foreign audience. An old man with a violin case chatted happily to the conductor, pulling his empty pocket linings out in just the way Des had done to Sayid. Then he seated himself, legs wide, set his fiddle under his chin and began to play. Those whose hands were occupied with shopping stamped to the rhythm instead of clapping. A middle-aged woman with a pear-shaped golden face leaned back in her seat and began to sing, a wild, wordless music full of pain and ardour. They were, in their own way, as moving as the professional gipsy musicians from the North.

Ten minutes along their way Paula was amused to see the New Zealand quartet get on accompanied by Colonel Martin and Cynth. The fiddler now put away his violin and sat rigidly to attention, his fare adequately covered. The other passengers ran their dark eyes over the newcomers like inquisitive ants. Certainly they were worthy of attention, seeming so foreign in this setting, and individual almost to the point of caricature.

The men's appearance was rapidly dismissed. It was, naturally, the women who were being feasted on. Neurotics such as the Colonel's wife were quite alien, but then Cynth, as Paula now knew, had spent her war in a Jap prison camp, while the atrocities on Crete had been more sudden and final. Mrs Scott went across as a minuscule Great Lady— they should have seen Mrs Van L as she set off this morning! —but it was the twins who stole the scene.

Gaynor was demure in pink figured voile with a white silk headscarf tucked round her blonde curls. Michaela, in vivid green and purple, was a female leprechaun gone punk.

The bus's romping and the loud Cretan voices made conversation impossible. Paula smiled the length of the bus, waved her fingers and resumed her interest in the passing scenery. She got out a little short of Rethymnon's limits before the others had collected themselves together. Wandering at her ease through the old streets, lunching on *moussaka*, yogurt and wine, then walking back along the long shore of golden sand, she had forgotten them completely until she stumbled on a recognizable pink voile confection discarded on a tamarisk. Of Gaynor Scott there was no other evidence, but rounding an outcrop of rock she came on her grunting and moaning in the sand.

The girl's hands were scrabbling and her eyes tight closed. The man she was wrapped about barely glanced up, then redoubled his efforts. Paula walked carefully round them and on towards the sea.

There was a sheltered bay beyond, and here she caught up with Michaela sitting hunched on a flat rock, twitchy and darting her lizard-glance over one shoulder, uncommunicative as she rolled herself a joint.

'Do you mind if I swim here?' Paula demanded. Michaela shrugged and watched unmoved as Paula stripped down to her pants. Here the topless rule held good, and anyway who was here to see her? The bikini would keep for later when she'd dried off in the sun. She pushed her dress and the tote bag into a tidy heap with her toes, nodded and walked into the sea.

Each to his own taste, she thought, carrying with her the other girl's hostile stare which warned, *Make trouble if you dare!* She swam out with slow, powerful strokes, then turned on her back to float, closing her eyes against the brilliant sky.

Crete was a long way to come for what one could find at home: Gaynor for instant coupling with a stranger, Michaela for hash, the Canadian Widows for bridge and gold bangles, Malcolm Bowles seeking out his little catamite. What diverse options offered by a holiday. And what had Foden said about dragging your Hell around inside you? Had she done the same herself?

No, she'd come looking for the past, for the Knossos of her father, found it, sloughed it off and now was more free. Ready for whatever the future had to offer.

She shook drops of water from her face, and her hair floated wide like black seaweed about her. The sun warmed her through as the water gently rocked her. Life was very, very good.

CHAPTER 12

Despite his weariness Angus was ready for action. In the hotel at Iraklion there was already a message waiting for him. He tore it open eagerly. The local police, warned by Athens of his coming, would pick him up tomorrow at 09.00 hours. Tomorrow! Office hours! What the hell were they doing right now? Already belching over their suppers?

Angus glared his frustration. Before such anger the little Front Desk Manager quailed. He had instructions to keep this guest satisfied, and above all quiet. He twisted the room key between his neat, slender fingers. 'It is the same room,' he murmured. 'Her room. By special request of the Kápetan.'

'Kápetan?'

'The Kápetan of Police here, who writes your letter. I take you up now.'

This attention wasn't necessary, but perhaps the man could tell him something, though from his delicacy and the use he made of his eyelashes he'd more likely remember the men than the women.

As they rode up in the lift the policeman in Angus automatically registered *top floor*; *entrance to roof garden*; *her door positioned where all comings and goings could be observed*. Did something happen to her because she saw someone or something meant to be kept secret? That was one possibility. He'd need to check on her neighbours.

Inside, it was just a hotel bedroom, empty, tidied for its new occupant, totally anonymous. 'Did she leave anything behind?' he demanded. 'Anything at all?'

The beautiful young man turned his palms outwards. Embarrassed, he let the dark eyelashes drop on his soft cheeks. 'The police have been here—discreetly, of course—but they found nothing.'

'Who was next door?'

'On this side, the linen room. On the other, an elderly English lady, Miss Pallett. She is very—correct, do you say?'

Angus stared at the twin beds. 'Single guests in double rooms. Bad for business.'

'We charge a small supplement. Some people like to be alone. Others have friends who—'

'Who drop in. Quite.'

'Not Miss Musto. I asked the chambermaid. Only one bed ever used. And it is not so big, see?'

Angus thought he saw. It was how he would expect it to be with Paula. She hadn't come on holiday to pick up a lover.

'You will eat now, Inspector? I have it sent up for you. And our best wine.'

'Whatever you have. Something cold, but later.'

'I send up also the girl who does the room. She comes back specially. For the famous detective from London.' Sinuous movements of the delicate hands, and the eyes wide with admiration.

'Thank you. I'll see her first. Then the guests. There is nothing you can tell me?'

'I see the young lady come and go, always a smile. She have many friends. Everyone like Miss Musto. No one special, I think. She like to be alone.' The little Manager shrugged his regrets. 'About the guests, they do not know she disappear. They do not expect the police.' His eyes pleaded for discretion. Angus nodded and the man left.

While he waited Angus prowled the room, the bathroom section, the generous balcony. This looked over a small square with a few palm trees as its centre. He went back and opened the wall cupboard, removed the drawers, inspected them underneath. Pointless to strip the bed when it had been completely remade and also suffered police examination. In any case, what would Paula need to conceal? There could be no hidden message for him unless she'd known she was to disappear.

The chambermaid spoke little English, so her husband, a waiter, came with her to interpret. Angus learned little from her but that Paula was 'pretty lady, very kind, speak some Greek words, leave room nice'. Paula had definitely used the room on her last night here and put out her luggage for the coach.

If this woman was typical of the staff here it could well be true what the Manager claimed: that the guests still didn't know anything untoward had happened. They were isolated by their foreignness, just as he was. He'd learn only what these Cretans chose to put into English.

He had little more luck with the waiter, Lavros, who had several times served her meals. The man was squat, dark, Neanderthal, with black hair over the back of his hands. Having no servile qualities, no doubt his value lay in his energy and an ability to shout his orders to the chef louder than the next man. He too thought Paula a 'very nice lady' but he also praised her way of dressing, her choice of menu, her conversation. Just an exuberant attempt to get a larger tip. Nothing of any use. Like the Manager, he said she moved equally among the Fiesta party, cultivated no one more than another.

Alone, Angus thought. Slightly aloof, so not involved, and possibly, because of that, more observant? Picking up items of information that others missed, and so endangering herself? Could it be that? If so, what had been going on here? It was time to meet her companions, such as remained.

There was a tap at his door and he opened it on a large, expansive young man with hair springing wildly from his crown and flopping between spectacles and eyes. 'Mr Mott,' he said at once, 'ah'm Andy Whitelaw. The powers-that-be have sent me in to be of assistance if I can. Ah'm the Fiesta rep.'

'Responsible for your clients' safe-keeping,' Angus accused him grimly.

'Aw, don't rub it in. Ah feel awfu', I do really. Such a nice wee gurrl, so interested in everything. Verra keen on the tours, such as she went on. Ah think she was legging it a lot too, and making use of local buses. Look, ah've brought a list of the places we went, and ah've marked the trips she was on.'

Angus faced him. 'So what do you think happened?'

'Ah've no idea at a'. There's no crime on Crete, y'know. An accident somewhere, on her own. Or if she met someone not too pleasant—another tourist, I mean—well, you can't really tell.'

'So when and where did you last see her?'

'Ah've been thinking about tha'. She was on the coach from here that last morning, because ah did a careful head count. One missing at first, but that was Mr Donaldson held up by a phone ca'. Then, at the airport—' Andy scratched his brow and frowned.

'Pretty chaotic?'

'Always is. Ah can't honestly say ah remember her taking her boarding card off me, but ah did see her over at the carousel. They had to identify their big luggage as it came off the coach and put it themselves on the moving track.'

'What colour case?' Angus checked.

The courier closed his eyes. 'Wait now. Red. She'd two, matching. That's how ah noticed her right across the hall.'

'You're sure that's who it was?'

'Well, who else would it be? Black hair, red cases. Yes.' Angus didn't dispute this: a credible bit of recognition-shorthand such as couriers might well employ. 'Can you come down now and show me which of the guests were here last week?'

'Surely. Of course, quite a few went back the same day as she did.'

'Such as Kate Drummond.'

'Aye. She was one of the frisky leddies from Toronto. They're all away now. Your Miss Musto got on verra well with a' that lot.'

'Are you sure? I met Mrs Drummond in Athens and she didn't remember Paula.'

'Not by name mebbe. She's a poor one at names. Had her own label for nearly everyone. Things she could recall them by. No one minded. Now wha' was it she called your young leddy? Aye, *Tangerine*. If you'd said "Tangerine" she'd a' known well enough.'

'Why Tangerine?'

'Heaven alone knows. A substitute for "Peach" or "Honey"?'

'You might have something there. Let's go now and meet the Fiesta crowd before they get any ideas about going to bed early.'

They found most of the original party in the card lounge. Wednesday's newcomers, who didn't concern Angus, were mainly non-bridge players and had congregated in the bar. This made it simpler to infiltrate, although Andy Whitelaw had to wade through numerous complaints and requests before he had Angus generally presented as a latecomer to the Fiesta programme. He refused the invitation to take someone's place in a rubber, and sat apart sharing a bottle of wine with the courier and getting a low-voiced run-down on the players.

'All the regular bridge-fiends are here,' Andy summed up, 'except the two Belgian leddies who're away with the Hungarian doctor and her son. The last two aren't with Fiesta but live in rooms in Iraklion, as does Mr Foden there.' He nodded across at a lean, sardonic man in his fifties partnering the New Zealand woman against Colonel Martin and the Miss Pallett whose room was next to Paula's.

'Your young leddy spent quite a lot of time with the Van Leidens too, but they left a couple of days before she did. A mother and young son. They're in Athens now.'

'The son Paula's age?'

'No. Eleven or twelve. Could be sassy on occasion, but she had the measure of him. If you want someone nearer to her in age you should try Mrs Bowles over there or the Scott twins, daughters of the New Zealand couple.'

'Where are they?'

'Probably dancing in the main lounge.'

'Let's go through, then.'

It was a disco number and a couple of dozen people were stomping and jerking to an old Spandau Ballet tape. A half-hearted attempt at strobe lighting dappled the moving figures with flickers of purple, red and green. When the music and the revolutions stopped he saw that one girl remained unchanged, being herself a punk version of strobe camouflage. She came over with a long, twitchy stride, hands in pockets of Sinbad pants, a magenta and black blouse worn off one shoulder and a yellow silk butterfly in her spiked, baize-green hair. 'This is Michaela Scott,' Andy explained. 'Michaela, meet Angus Mott.'

'Mott-and-Scott, Scott-and-Mott,' repeated Michaela with the same obsessive rhythm as the music. She clicked her fingers for a metronome. 'No-o, no-o, not on at a-all.'

'And this,' the courier continued unabashed, 'is Michaela's twin sister Gaynor.'

'Let's say it for him. One-two-three-four, "Ooh, you're not alike, are you?"' Michaela mocked him. Gaynor smiled, showing neat, perfectly white teeth.

'Hallo, Gaynor,' said Angus, relieved to find someone who approximated to a real feminine girl. 'Would you like to dance?'

'Smooch music,' Michaela crowed as the new tape began. She gave him a convulsive monkey-grimace, staring after them as they moved off together.

'Let's go outside,' Gaynor pleaded as they completed one circuit of the lounge. Angus hadn't thought his dancing all that bad, but he welcomed an opportunity to question the girl. There must have been times when she was in Paula's company, perhaps even shared her confidence. They went out now on to the wide steps behind the hotel and into the shadowed square.

'I'd hoped to see a friend of mine here,' he had begun, when he realized that Gaynor had reasons of her own for withdrawal from the lighted public rooms. She was nudging him, her fingers wantonly fondling, exploring. Simultaneously he felt his body respond and the hairs along his spine bristle like an indignant dog's.

'Angus,' Gaynor said wonderingly, and reached up to pull his face down to her own.

'Why,' he asked, firmly resisting, 'don't you let me buy you a *moussaka* or something? I won't be eaten. I want to talk, about Paula Musto. Remember her?'

'No,' murmured Gaynor, shaking her pretty curls and pouting like a Victorian miss. Her fingers resumed stiffly walking down his shirtfront.

'Did you happen to see her leave last Wednesday?'

'See who leave?' At last he seemed to be getting through to her. She frowned helpfully.

'Paula. My girl. I was delayed and I've missed her somehow.'

Gaynor laughed breathlessly. 'So she's not here. Hard cheese! You'll have to make do—'

Angus treated her to a sharp four-letter comment and forcibly restrained her. From behind he heard a little malicious chuckle. Michaela, in fixed angular pose against an ornate pillar, leered at him. 'Paula's man? Miss Icicle herself?'

Play it cool, Angus warned himself. He smiled. 'Depends on how much you know about thermal interaction,' he said mildly. 'What's your theory?'

Michaela jerked herself into a new pose, aggressive now. 'Ask Gaynor. That's *her* line.'

Angus looked at her shrewdly. 'And you're anything that's the opposite, yes?'

'Slob!' she threatened him, her painted face thrust up against his own.

'Okay, so I'm wise to you,' he said gently. 'So now help me, will you? I'm hellish worried, because Paula didn't reach home. She matters a lot to me, and I have to find her before anything bad happens.'

He hadn't misjudged the girl. The sharp little face softened. Her eyes, inside the punk make-up, went quite round. 'Well, she's left here. Otherwise we'd have seen her.'

'When was the last time you did?'

'I'd have to think.'

'At Rethymnon,' Gaynor said suddenly. 'She nearly walked on me in the sand. I was—'

'Shut up,' Michaela commanded. She turned to Angus. 'That was on Monday. I saw her next morning just as she went off with Frau Dok and the reptile son. The Petitjean came rushing up and demanded her passport. God knows what for.'

'For Andy Whitelaw to check because they were leaving next morning?'

'Only *Paula* was from that group. The Belgians have another week. But Petitjean didn't hand the passport in for her at the desk. She went upstairs and when she came down she went straight out to the car. I noticed because usually the Frau Dok hires one complete with chauffeur. This time the Petitjean got in behind the wheel herself, and the others were in back.'

'Which others?'

'All the gang. Frau Dok, the son, Paula. No, wait. Frau Dok was up front. Just Paula and Jozsef behind. For some reason Sylvie wasn't there that time.'

'She was sick that day. She didn't join them till Wednesday,' said Gaynor sulkily.

'Who are Petitjean and Sylvie?'

Michaela explained and he nodded. 'Yes, Andy mentioned two Belgians. And that's really the last you saw of Paula? Nothing on Wednesday?'

The twins looked at each other. For the first time Angus realized they were identical under their distinctive disguises.

'Maybe she didn't come back Tuesday night?' Michaela sounded doubtful.

Angus shook his head. 'The chambermaid said she used her room. And her luggage was put out as instructed. But somewhere en route she disappeared.' He was loath, for some reason, to admit to them that a substitute had ended in her place.

'Then why are you *here*? Isn't the key to it all at the airport? Or in Athens?'

'Athens! Of course. That's where the Van Leidens went.' Gaynor sounded triumphant.

It comes back to that, Angus thought starkly. The action being elsewhere, and he'd let that smart-shirt Athens Security Chief sidetrack him to Crete where the trail had long gone cold.

He went back and mingled when the bridge party broke up, letting drop that he knew Paula, had intended meeting her, and gradually the notion circulated that he was worried and needing information about her departure. Nobody had actually seen her at breakfast on Wednesday, but if she'd gone out early that wasn't surprising. Miss Pallett, for some reason looking affronted, admitted to hearing her move about in the next room, but she hadn't looked out when the door was finally shut. Angus wondered what Paula had done to put the old trout off.

Back in his own room he threw his clothes off, left the balcony door open to the warm night air, and stared out at the scene which must have been familiar to Paula. There

were little pools of light in the square below where people
were sitting, and now he noticed the smaller courtyards, the
tiny patios with sagging thatch or tangled vine roof crammed
between the older type, squat houses with flaking stucco
painted in thick pastels. Dead opposite some shops were
still lit, and it seemed there were late workers catching up
in certain offices above. At one point there was a party in
full swing on the roof, with Chinese lanterns slung between
potted shrubs, and a barrel of wine as focal point.

When he stretched out on the unopened bed his fatigue
hit him like a blow between the eyes. He was almost instantly
asleep and slept heavily on until after daybreak.

He surfaced through a sensation of being with Paula. He
could see her sitting with him on the balcony, steadily
nodding as he spoke to her. But he couldn't hear his own
voice, couldn't guess at the words. And the balcony was
wrong, having a sort of blue trellis with a vine growing up
it, and the floor was bare, sandy rock. He thought he heard
the sea whispering in the background, but as his eyes came
open he recognized human speech. In the corridor outside
there was the clink of keys on a ring, then someone entering
next door.

The linen room, he remembered. These were the
chambermaids coming on early duty. He slipped a pre-
cautionary lock on the door and went through to take a
shower. Ten minutes later, in sandals, jeans and sports shirt,
he ran down to make a phone call.

The telephone system was one of Crete's pleasant sur-
prises, like the new inter-city roads. Adequate and efficient.
Wherever you spotted the little red instrument—in hotel
lobbies, at kiosks in the open street—you had international
dialling direct. Just have enough drachmas and you were
through to Tokyo, Washington, Jakarta, London. He
phoned from under a plastic bubble in the entrance hall,
beside the fresco of a rampant Minotaur. The call went well
as far as Mike's office, then an unknown voice said sorry,

Detective-Superintendent Yeadings was away. He'd left no message for Angus.

Nothing for it but to try the Guv's home number. Nan, briefed in advance, answered and the sound of her voice, warm and concerned, steadied him. Mike, she said, had scrounged a bit of leave, flew out last night to Frankfurt-on-Main. There was no development yet and he wasn't expecting to do more than point out a few directions before he was due to get back. He had Angus's number at the hotel at Iraklion. Was there anything moving at his end?

Big zero, he told her. The sun burned holes in the pavement and no one knew anything. He hadn't solved her final diary jotting: *Goodbye drinks at K's.* It could refer to almost anyone.

In Reading, England, Nan countered, they'd had rain all night but the sun was just about to struggle through.

Same sun. Same big zero.

Nan Yeadings sighed as she put back the receiver. Angus had forgotten the two hours' difference between England and Crete. Here it was coming up to 6 a.m. The phone's ringing had woken Sally too. Nan could hear her moving about on the landing, organizing her family of fluffy toys. She started coming down now, a pop-eyed furry owl under one arm. 'Oliver's hungry.' The blunt little features screwed up to indicate it was a joke. Eleven years and seven months of human experience locked up in Down's Syndrome.

'He'd better have his breakfast, then. Shall we too?'

'Yes. Daddy phone?'

'No. That was Angus. He's up specially bright and early.'

'So's Oliver.'

'Wise old owl.' She busied herself making toast while Sally happily made plopping noises to encourage the percolator. They had almost finished their breakfast washing-up when the phone rang again.

'Daddy.'

'Maybe. Better let me take it, love. It could start off in German.'

But the voice and language were English. Nan recognized her caller from their conversation of the previous evening. 'Sorry it's a bit early,' said Paula's flatmate Lottie. 'Got a train to catch—going to visit a power station—and I thought you'd want the answer right away.' Lottie was a woman engineering student.

'Was the luggage list any good?'

'I think so. Checked it over with what's left in her wardrobe here. There's one outfit definitely missing. Quite spectacular: black silk camisole top with a tangerine gathered skirt which has a black key pattern round the hem. Not at all run-of-the-mill.'

'That should help, if Paula had it on when—'

'Quite,' Lottie agreed gruffly. 'Only thing is, though—'

'Yes?' Nan caught the hesitance and guessed the girl was a long way from the detachment her abrupt manner suggested.

'Knowing Paula, well, not the sort of thing she'd travel in. Bare shoulders and that. She had a sort of linen trouser suit for the plane. Willow green. That was included on your list, so she'd packed it.'

Nan remembered the suit because she'd watched the suitcases opened at Heathrow. Everything had been carefully packed, the dresses and skirts meticulously folded; soiled clothes separate in a plastic laundry bag. But the pale green trouser suit had been rolled up and stuffed in at the sides, as if at the last moment.

'Yes, I see.' Well, maybe somebody else had finished the packing, the trouser suit an afterthought, not needed for the journey because Paula wouldn't be travelling herself after all. 'Thanks, Lottie. That could be significant.'

'Ominous,' Lottie said abruptly. 'No news, I suppose?'

'Nothing yet. I'll let you know, if and when.'

Lottie said goodbye hurriedly, no doubt bound for her

train. Nan wrote out the information on the telephone pad, using Lottie's own words as far as possible. Mike always said it was detail that mattered. The mosaic, and then *having the nose*, knowing what to disregard.

She wondered what he was doing now. In Frankfurt it would be nine-seventeen, well into a policeman's working day, and the Germans were sticklers for punctuality.

CHAPTER 13

The police car was waiting at two minutes short of the hour. Its uniformed driver checked his name but offered no conversation on the short journey down a main street and off at a turning by a large Byzantine church. A clerical officer took Angus directly up to the Kápetan's office where a massive man stood leaning with palms flat on a desk, in the stance of one delivering a prepared address.

He might have the body of a gigantic and self-indulgent toad, but there was nothing soft about the face that stared across at Angus. Pock-marked and sun-dried, it was harsh as a sandstone quarry. He greeted the visitor briefly, nodding him into a chair.

'My concern is Security,' he opened. 'Your countrymen regard "security" as no more than the collateral offered against a loan of money. For us it is more. It is the means of physical survival.'

He stood straight to continue. 'Foreigners see us as a political people. We are not so much political as geographically aware. There are dangerous pressures from the countries we lie between—Albania, Yugoslavia, Bulgaria, Turkey, Libya.'

He sighed and slumped into his seat. 'Our enlightened government has a policy of open friendship to all. We must forget the past; forget fellow Greeks made homeless by invaders in Cyprus, regular violations of our territorial waters by gunboats, continual attempts to corrupt our young people by the landing of illicit drugs. We must regard the Bulgarians as potentially gentle neighbours; contrive not to notice Qaddafi's factories for international terrorism barely two hundred miles south of our island.

'Give no offence: that is the edict from Athens, and my colleagues and I are trained to obey authority. Otherwise we could wield none ourselves.'

The Policeman's Lot, Angus noted. Here, as elsewhere, quite evidently Not a Happy One.

'But—' and here it comes—'there are types of visitor we do not encourage: who threaten us or our real friends. So we watch how our visitors conduct themselves, to ensure that they—and others—do not come to any harm.'

'Or go missing,' Angus said bluntly, to get things moving.

Momentarily the sandstone quarry looked even craggier, but the voice continued smoothly. 'So we take certain precautions, and do not act before we are certain of their standing. In your case, Mr Mott, I am satisfied—'

'That I am who I claim to be.'

'Precisely. My respected colleague, from England. The Kápetan inclined his head in an ironic bow. 'I welcome your concern for the young lady, deplore that she is not here to greet you in person, and am agog to discover what theories you can offer to account for her failure to arrive back in England.'

Agog, Angus marked up. The man's world-weary features displayed not even a polite imitation of interest. And his practised command of English betrayed him as political however much he might deny it. There followed then a gruelling cross-questioning about Paula, himself, and both their backgrounds. Angus gritted his teeth and endured it, sweating with anger. 'I too look forward to an exchange of information,' he concluded stiffly.

The edge of sarcasm wasn't lost on the other. He gave a

fierce smile. 'Unfortunately we know only what you have learned yourself, Mr Mott: that the young lady left Crete from Iraklion Airport at the conclusion of her stay, and on the flight she had intended to use. It is not surprising therefore—to myself at any rate—that you do not find her here.'

'Someone left on that flight,' Angus said grimly. 'Someone using her name, her passport, her tickets, and with her luggage. The luggage eventually reached London. On the way the impostor went missing herself, perhaps returned to her own identity. She hasn't been traced yet, but when she is there will be fresh inquiries directed through Interpol. We shall want to know above all where the real Paula Musto is, who conspired in the substitution, and who stood to gain by the fact of keeping it secret.'

The sandstone became granite, but the Kápetan's voice was gently sibilant. 'Suppositions, Mr Mott. You are, by training, a particularly suspicious person. Naturally you are upset that the young lady has—*disappointed* you. But perhaps with reflection you will accept that she could have had some private reason of her own—'

'Kápetan,' Angus said shortly, rising to go, 'it is an offence to use another's papers of identity. I am sure you do not take it lightly.'

The Greek Security man rose in his turn, outwardly polite. 'Rest assured, respected colleague, that if such a case were to occur, and be proved, it would be dealt with most severely.'

They eyed each other a long moment. The Kápetan gave a small, stiff bow. They omitted to shake hands and Angus nodded back. Nothing achieved, he thought leadenly as he slogged back on foot to the hotel.

The sun was high. He was stinging with heat and his shirt stuck damply between his shoulder-blades. Rebuffed and ruffled, fit for no more than wound-licking, Angus slid into the gloom of the Maze Bar and looked around, on his guard against cheerful approaches from any Fiesta acquaintances.

There was only one figure he recognized, and no conversational threat to judge by his brevity at their earlier meeting. Huddled on a bar stool, his right hand protectively about the remains of a brandy, Foden was nevertheless treating a submissive stranger to a treatise on *The Brits, What is Wrong With Them*. The difference, Angus saw, was the inspirational alcofluence of incohol, less marked at their first encounter. Now Foden's voice was on autopilot, monotonously projecting some deeply sited pre-recording. He had reached that godlike state of detachment when he spoke of his fellow countrymen as 'them'.

'Know the big mistake?' he demanded, pressing his one-man audience who was too civil or too thirsty to make his escape, 'Sold themselves short all along the line. Apologized, for God's sake, for their own suc-successes. Went on and on about what poor oafs they were, inefff-fectual amateurs muddling along. Came another generation, more factual, used to hearing what pukes the British were, they got to believe it. Gave up trying. Now if you point to a p-positive achievement, the best anyone thinks is it's an accident or they're a nation of have-beens.'

'Oh now, I wouldn't say that,' rumbled a Midwestern voice in faint protest. The man blinked hopefully towards Angus who had no intention of helping him off the hook.

'And you Yanks,' Foden pursued, slotting in another reel of prejudice, 'same thing. Worse even, because you're shovelling in dollars all the while. Every film, every book, every day on television, all the world over. Selling yourselves as rotten to the core. Bent cops, crooked presidents, Mafia hi-hierarchies, power-mad oilmen, corrupted sewer-rats for Senators. Wallowing in your own crap, right? Who's going to believe anyone clean's left living?'

He bent close and aimed a forefinger at the other. 'D'you know the two words tailormade to sell your fiction? *Shit* and *fuck*. Whose fault if the world thinks that's all you can do?'

The Midwesterner stuck out his chin and drew a loud

breath. His polite, good-natured face had been squaring and steadily darkening under its holiday tan. A tirade against the Brits he was prepared to endure and mildly refute. The honour of the US of A was something else entirely.

'He's drunk,' he said tightly to Angus, slid from his stool and went out with the march of a middle-aged ex-Marine.

'Single Metaxa and a filter coffee,' Angus told the barman. He waited while the drink was measured and the machine hissed out steaming water into a double pottery cup. Foden had retreated seemingly into an inner, silent monologue.

'You have an interesting theory,' Angus offered. 'The two key words of US Lit. So which are the obligatory two that sell British fiction?'

The man turned his head to face him, the green, slightly protuberant eyes glazed with inexpressible misery. 'Piss—off,' he said in a voice empty of all feeling.

It could have been an answer, or merely a reaction. Whichever, Angus couldn't fault it. The incident would have been comic but for the man's eyes when at last they didn't evade him. Foden was a disaster.

Angus took his two drinks over to a dark corner of the room and slid behind a table. The shade had been deceptive. It was hotter here because the ceiling fan didn't reach far enough to circulate the used air. He swallowed the coffee scalding hot and chased it with the brandy, then sat back to enjoy his pores unloading. Maybe along with the sweat and heat a few ideas would surface.

He watched Foden unhook his heels carefully from the bar stool and try them on the floor. With tense concentration the man steered for the door and went out. Angus crossed to take the next stool and pushed over his cup for a refill. 'He's started early,' he commented.

The barman stared unresponsively back. He was a big fellow, half way to a Japanese wrestler, but the embedded eyes were wary like a male gorilla's. 'Mr Foden,' he offered at length, bringing a fresh cup for the filter coffee, 'has a sorrow. Also he is sad for your friend. He thinks she goes with the lost ones.'

'And this makes him drink?'

'What else to do? For him it is too late.'

Angus Mott looked hard at the man. He had moved away and was slowly polishing the metal trim of the rear counter, but he gave the impression of waiting to be called back. For questioning? About Paula?

'My friend, Miss Musto,' Angus prompted. 'You met her, of course.'

'She come in the bar.' The man rubbed harder, spoke over his shoulder. 'Two times when I am working here. I see her once at the harbour besides.'

'When was that?'

'Saturday night, a week gone.'

The excitement that had been building up in Angus dispersed. What help was Saturday when she'd disappeared four days later?

'She is with gipsies, dancing, very happy.' Damn the man, he knew only the present tense in English. *Was* with the gipsies, of course. *Had been happy*.

'Then she leave them, and I think she look for the lost ones. They dance, besides.'

That was the second time he'd used the expression. Some specific people then? '*The lost ones?*'

Now the man turned to face him, his big face puckered. 'The young people who—' He tapped his head gently.

'Tell me about them.' He listened while the barman explained about the communes. He didn't mention drugs, but he didn't need to for Angus. It was part of the recognizable pattern. Every country had them, the easy dupes of the big-money men who leeched on boredom and desperation, sold them early death.

'But she does not meet them,' the barman assured him. 'I watch, because I have daughters too. She come back here.

I follow all the way. Perhaps she know I follow, but not see me. I come in the hotel at back.'

Angus eyed the big man. It would have scared Paula, being tailed. She had been mugged once, in London, and scented that sort of danger quickly. Yet there'd been no mention of it in her diary. He must look at Saturday again. 'The lost ones,' he insisted. 'Why does Mr Foden fear she may be with them?'

The barman looked around for something else to work on. Angus had to wait while he made up his mind to speak. 'He has a son, come from England. Mr Foden come after but soon the son die. Now Mr Foden has a sorrow and he stay here.'

Foden, poor devil, must have thrown up his job, whatever, come here to save the boy, found him too far gone, stayed on to the bitter end and now was stranded without any motive or the power to do anything but face one day after the other as it came. Small wonder he drank or indulged his bitter humour at bridge when he steeled himself to confront human society again. 'When was this?' Angus asked.

'A year gone. Few people know. No visitors.' It was a warning to discretion. Angus had been admitted to the secret because he too had trouble of the same kind. He nodded. 'Where do I go to find the lost ones?'

The man looked distressed. 'I think your friend is not with them.'

'I have to make sure. It's the only lead so far.'

'Ask Mr Foden. He know. They move between villages, but sometimes they talk to him.'

It was all the barman was going to give him. Perhaps he already regretted revealing so much about a customer he had feeling for and respected. The man moved away, deadpan, to serve a quartet of Swiss who had just come in demanding ices. Angus made himself relax, plucked the shirt off his skin and felt a watery trickle run down his spine.

The soft background of *bouzouki* music was cut off and he

heard his name called. 'Mr Mott, telephone please, in the entrance hall.' His hopes flared. He peeled off a couple of hundred-drax notes and strode out.

It was the Guv, phoning from Frankfurt, just on the point of flying back to London.

'Briefly, lad, there's a small item from each port of call. Here they've turned up Paula's passport, stuffed down the side of a refuse bin behind the Hotel Bristol. Proof positive, they'll agree now, that it wasn't young Paula who travelled here last Wednesday. Then Kostantinou from Athens has made some discreet inquiries through the Antoniades Corporation. Paula's friend Dímitra was suddenly called north to deliver some documents to her father, so phoned Paula in Iraklion to cancel their rendezvous between Paula's planes. A stroke of luck for the impostor, because otherwise it might have caught her out. The third point is one for you to work on. Lottie, at Paula's flat, checked the luggage contents. There's an outfit missing: black top—"camisole", Nan calls it—and orange skirt. D'you know it?'

'Yes, go on.'

'She'd meant to travel in a green trouser suit, which was crammed in at the end. Everything else folded carefully. Any significance?'

Not orange, Angus thought suddenly. Tangerine! That's what Kate Drummond called her. 'I'm almost sure the black and orange things were here,' he said quickly. 'Maybe she's still wearing them. Should be easy to pick out. Thanks, Guv. I'll work on it. I've seen the local police, but no go. Ball-crushing, in fact.'

Yeadings was silent a moment. 'You're on the wrong side of the counter, lad. That's all. They won't be idle, and you've got to accept you're suspect. We'd play it much the same here.'

'For God's sake, I'm trying to help.'

'Carry on, lad. I've got a plane to catch now. Keep on looking. Nan sends love, Sally too,'

The passport, Angus thought as he replaced the receiver; it would be undergoing searching forensic tests in Frankfurt, but unless the girl who used it was a professional criminal any fingerprints raised wouldn't lead anywhere. It was the missing tangerine skirt that offered most.

He crossed the entrance hall and found Andy Whitelaw beside the lifts pinning a paper on the Fiesta noticeboard. He grinned with bonhomie, then wiped the cheerfulness off, out of respect for the occasion. 'Any news yet?'

Angus opened up and confessed he was snookered. Then he passed on the Guv's three items.

'Oh Lord,' Andy said wearily. 'Ah don't like that passport business at all. It sounds a mighty sight too final.'

'The *tangerine* skirt,' Angus prompted.

'Ah remember it now. Aye, that'll be what Mrs Drummond called her after.'

'Do you remember it in the airport on Wednesday, or in the coach going there?'

The courier thought, then shook his head. 'Two coaches of fifty people. They were just heads to be counted. Didn't exist otherwise. Later I recall the red cases and black hair, nothing more. She could've been standing behind someone big and just reaching forward. Aye, that's how it was. Ah'm verra sorry.'

'She'd meant to travel in a green trouser suit. Why would she suddenly change her mind?'

'Too hot? Spilt something on the suit? Was going somewhere first and meant to change back, ran short of time at the end?'

'But why two outfits so early in the day?'

'Aw, *women*. Who understands their attitude to clothes? Maybe she was going to see someone who liked that tangerine outfit specially, or recognized her by it?'

'I could ask in the shops round here,' Angus said slowly. 'Someone might recall seeing her that morning.'

'Why not? They speak English nearly everywhere. I'd help out but I've a load—'

'Okay. Thanks for what you've done.' Angus waved a hand, hunched his shoulders and made for outdoors. 25th August Street, he decided, where the shops were, then Daedalos Street. After that, Eleftherías Square and something to eat.

Tantalizingly ephemeral ahead of him, weaving through the throng of shoppers, he thought he saw occasionally the girl he'd first taken out to supper in Soho after he'd caused her to drop a box of eggs. Same lovely girl, same black silk top, tangerine skirt (new on for the occasion, she'd admitted later; to impress him. Such an impression that the ghost lived on forever in his mind).

He tried desultorily picking on shops that might have attracted her. Some assistants recalled the face in the photograph, some remembered the bright skirt which he described. Nobody could definitely say when they'd last seen her.

It began to look hopeless. That was a well-known stage in house-to-house inquiries. You reached it, slogged on through it and continued regardless. A frustration warp. Beyond it there was sometimes luck.

He came out of the tobacconist's. (Paula didn't smoke but she might have bought Greek cigars for the Guv or Lottie's man, Horace.) The next place was a camera shop advertising Kodak.

Paula had packed a camera! It hadn't been listed in her luggage contents and there'd been no mention of films, exposed or otherwise. On the offchance he went in and asked for prints ordered in the name of Musto. The pretty Cretan girl smiled nicely, ran her fingers through a box of bulging wallets and pulled out two secured with an elastic band. She looked at Angus doubtfully. '*Miss* Musto.'

'This lady,' and Angus showed her the photograph. He shelled out the drachmas he'd bought at the hotel exchange and took delivery of his first and only material clue. 'When did she intend to collect this?' he asked.

The girl pointed to a note pencilled on the top wallet. 'Wednesday, 8.30 a.m. at latest. So we had them ready Tuesday night. She brought them in the evening before.'

'And she never came.'

'It must be so.'

He pushed the bundle of prints down inside the breast pocket of his bush shirt. It seemed to strike deadly cold to his over-heated skin. He couldn't wait now to look at what he'd got. There was a *taverna* on the corner, spilling its chairs down a side alley. He found a clear space, ordered an espresso coffee and dealt the photographs over the table like a game of patience. Places (some he recognized from travel literature); a few pleasing compositions with people; one excellent close-up of Dímitra, more poised and sleek than the rebellious Women's Lib student he'd known in London. There was Delphi several times, veiled in rain, drenched in sun, and overhung by Parnassus; the Parthenon; some unknown acropolis with a ruined temple of whitish stone; Epidavros and the Corinth Canal; seven or eight of Knossos. National costumes on little girls, stiff-armed to accommodate the vivid, heavily embroidered skirts; *Evzons* in their strange ballet-dress uniform, Disney-footed, doing a weird high-stepping march before a massive gate; pictures of ships, boats, skiffs, from the palatial to the humbly homemade. In all, two 35mm films, with thirty-six frames to each. In fact seventy-three photographs because she'd squeezed an extra in, by starting the second reel early.

The last-numbered wasn't so good but repeated the previous frame, a long shot across the square from her balcony, taken against the sun. It was focused so that the foreground was muzzy, the distant building opposite distinct but rather dark. In the centre a window with someone in it. Someone bending forward. Snapping him snapping her?

He wondered what made her take those two shots. Was

it only to finish off the roll? Or had they significance? In either case it was likely that she'd done it Monday afternoon and put the exposed films in for developing that evening, her last chance to get it done at the cheaper Greek price. When he'd had lunch he'd go and look for that window in Paula's picture, see what was so special about it.

CHAPTER 14

Back in his hotel room Angus set up Paula's last two photographs, and when he had identified the window at which the camera had been directed, he counted its position up from ground level and along from the corner. Then he went out into the sunlit square and sauntered across to the modern block opposite.

Behind a short arcade there was an internal lift shaft with access to all floors and a glass-panelled tubular lift. Off this were galleries with a mixture of boutiques and offices. At the fourth door on the third floor a notice was taped with the word 'Closed' in six languages. This bore out the evidence of the tilted venetian blinds he'd observed from outside. Nevertheless he placed his head against the panel and listened. That there were no voices didn't mean that no watcher was posted there. He tried looking through the keyhole but something dark obscured it.

He moved the handle experimentally, considering whether to use a little persuasion on the lock. It was then that he heard movement behind him and turned to find an olive-skinned man with one hand inside the breast pocket of a creased linen suit.

'Papers,' the man ordered, flicking out a pass of some kind which included his photograph. The printing was all in Greek, but he had to be police. Angus sighed and produced his passport, which the man read through slowly and returned. He looked at Angus with interest as though meeting someone he'd heard much of. He then asked why Angus should be interested in property which was unoccupied. Had he any intention of taking on the lease?

Angus smiled distantly and assured him that business was not in his mind. He'd had a whim merely to observe his hotel from here with a view to setting up a camera for photography.

The man's eyes flickered and Angus was satisfied he'd scored a hit. He allowed himself to be warned off, curious whether the man had been tailing him. It wouldn't be too difficult to ascertain, if he went round the block before returning to the hotel.

Satisfied that if the man had been shadowing him before he'd now given up, but further soured by his receiver-end view of police action, Angus went straight through to the Maze Bar and collected a half bottle of Minos. It was still siesta, so a slack time. The same big barman wanted to serve him at a table but he gestured to the doors open on to the terrace. 'I'll go out in the air.'

'Mr Foden is out there.' His voice gave no hint of whether that was warning or invitation.

Foden the Inebriate, Angus thought. Surly-sober or confiding-drunk. Maybe that was the sort of company he needed just now. 'What's he drinking?'

'Metaxa.'

'Pour him another. I'll take it out.' Angus walked into the staring light beyond the canopy. Foden sat slouched with a straw hat tipped over his eyes, a linen jacket discarded on the ground beside his chair.

'You'll find it too hot,' the man said as Angus's shadow fell across him.

'I can take a little heat.' The claim seemed more grimly true than he'd actually intended. He'd certainly been in the hot seat this morning with the Kápetan, and he'd had to take it, there being no alternative and no appeal. It had singed off him any idea of cooperation, but it made no difference to what he basically intended. It just meant he'd be alone in his search, have to use what resources came to hand and watch that he wasn't jockeyed into becoming *persona non grata* and sent back where he'd stand no chance of staying on the trail.

He grunted, pushing Foden's fresh glass towards him. He took the upturned wineglass off his bottle and carefully filled it for himself.

'Asbestine,' Foden said, enunciating carefully and watching him. 'And a man of few words. How did you get to be that way?'

'It comes with my job,' Angus said shortly.

Foden sat assessing him, the hat pushed back and one eyebrow quizzically cocked. His green eyes looked flatter now, like veined onyx, taking in the determined jawline and the athletic shoulders. 'Don't tell me. You're a fireman. Dedicated to the containment of volcanoes.'

Angus, untypically, swore, then gave a rueful grunt. 'And the trouble with volcanoes—'

'I know,' Foden agreed with feeling. 'I've lived in 'em.' Then, to cover over-exposed emotion, he smiled wryly. The eyebrows went more askew. 'And some of my best friends were little squirts.'

Angus considered him, the morose relic who became articulate when his high blood alcohol level was restored. 'What are *you* then?'

'I assume you mean professionally? We aren't getting metaphysical or whatever? I was a Civil Servant, for my sins. So altruistic and patriotically motivated that I opted for early retirement.' He smiled at the mock marbling of their laminate-topped table. 'I get in quite a bit of retiring, as no doubt you'll have the opportunity to observe. When I need to emerge I do it on this stuff.' He indicated the glass. 'I started off with the local *ouzo* when I first arrived, but I couldn't stand all the stray dogs following me around.

They go for the heaviest aniseed concentration, you know. Brandy they ignore. And it's cheap out here.'

That appeared to be the sum explanation of himself he intended to give, and even that he might regret offering once he completely sobered up. Angus felt he should reciprocate a little. 'Back home I'm a policeman,' he admitted.

'Good God, the Old Bill.' With exaggerated pernicker-tiness the older man removed his half-empty glass from propinquity with the other's. Fear of contagion, his mocking eyes said.

'I thought travel was supposed to broaden the out-look.'

'Perhaps, perhaps. I am willing to be forgiving. For the moment. If you'll tuck your handcuffs out of sight.'

'Small chance I'd have with any here,' Angus complained. 'I'm firmly on the offending side of the desk. Which has been made very plain. *That* tends to broaden the outlook.'

'Ah, very clean-shaven, dead-eyed, the local fuzz. I as-sume you refer to the hard boys, not the pretty tourist police.'

'The types down by the old Cathedral.'

'So they've had you down there? And you came back? It's a spider's parlour, by all accounts.'

'I went there to get help.'

'And they didn't want to know.'

'They wanted to know all right. They wanted to know the far end of a fart. I've met some intense interrogators. Their Kápetan was something more.'

'Orchestrated thumps and screams in the mid-distance? The titillating glimpse of lead-filled rubber? The odd elec-trode left lying about, tarnished brown stains on the floor-boards? No, surely just décor now, they tell me.'

'Nothing of the sort. Very correct. But just as you said—clean-shaven and dead-eyed. Relentless going over of the facts. I was minced. And then told to push off, keep my nose clean, leave it to them.'

Foden stared hard at him. 'They used to execute the bearer of bad news,' he said shrewdly.

'It was much like that. They had me little short of hanged for something ignored by them until I shoved it under their noses.'

'And sent you away charged with guilt about something you'd gone through hell for.' Foden's gaze was distant now, his face strangely taut, bitter with remembered pain. Still suffering it. His recovery this time was slower. He downed the last of his drink with an absent kind of disdain, then slowly turned to observe Angus's wretchedness. 'It's not so good on the receiving end, eh?'

Angus stared back. There was a new tone in the man's voice. He hadn't jeered, he'd prodded. Angus accepted the question as a serious inquiry and replied on the same level. 'To a policeman the experience isn't quite new. There are disciplinary inquiries, mats to be stood on. This is different. I went for help. I met a blank wall.'

'The mental half-nelson.' Foden nodded owlishly. 'They can't help themselves. They have a harsh reputation. They don't know if they have to live up to it or live it down. Between the devil and the deep blue sea. I don't want to pry, but I think we have trod the same path.'

Angus stared down at his own fingers locked tensely in his lap. He felt himself on the brink of confiding, although conscious still that this man was totally unreliable, at best a bit of cynical middle-aged flotsam he might otherwise have scorned but for this present need for human reassurance.

And then the opportunity was lost. A shadow came between them and the sun. The table lurched as a young man in cut-off faded jeans leant his weight on it. His long hair and matted beard were bleached near-white but his body was teak-coloured, long and emaciated, with patches of dry scale edged with angry red on ribs and shoulders. 'Friend,' he said to Angus, 'where you from?'

The policeman stared back unanswering.

'So,' the young man decided, and waved a hand dismissively.

'Hallo, Miles,' Foden offered.

'You know my name, man. That's wunnerful, you know.'

'How are things, then?'

'Wondrous fair, man. Sometimes. Sometimes not.'

'And the writing?'

The young man removed his weight from his arms and stiffly stood erect. 'The words flow.' He stared at his right hand as though they might even now visibly emerge from it and rush to record themselves on paper. 'No,' he denied, suddenly scowling, 'the words have gone. I paint. I dig my fingers in the pots and make wunnerful worlds to live in.'

Foden was groping for his discarded linen jacket. 'Have you enough—paints?'

'No bread, man.'

'Here.' He pushed a wad of drachma notes into the young man's outstretched hand. 'Make beautiful pictures, Miles. Be creative. That's what it's all about.'

'Preddy drax,' Miles said, peering at the denominations. 'You touch me, man. What they call you? I got to remember.'

'Foden.'

He brought his face down close to the man's, eyes wide-staring. '*Foden?* That's surely some works band you have. Keep it tootin'.' The boy was already on a trip but still just able to lean out of his pretty pink balloon and discern non-travellers left below.

'We can still perform.' Foden nodded, eager to prolong contact, but the boy had moved on, drachmas in hand, stooping and swaying to some private music inaudible to others. Foden clenched his hands on the wine-slopped table, then began deliberately to open them again, staring as the long, fine fingers separated. He glanced apologetically at Angus.

'You know how he'll spend it,' Mott grated.

'*Ne, Kápetan.*' Foden nodded. 'He will meet a man off the ferry, or from the airport, and he will buy the only thing he has learned to value. And if your colleagues from down by the Cathedral don't pick him up first, he will find his way south and take it back to his friends. They try to share it equally. They do that because they are afraid of dying alone.'

The words were sobering enough; the level monotone chilled Angus more than he believed possible, already inured to the drug scene back home. 'Is that where they go to get lost—the south?'

'You haven't been there yet?' There's a coach tour from the hotel twice a week. I sometimes go myself, to remind myself of my respectable background, and that I don't belong with the young.' He had drunk enough to be depressively talkative, perhaps not quite enough to be useless. Angus leaned towards him.

'You like young people. You mind what happens to them.'

Foden had slid down farther in his chair. 'They aren't like us,' he muttered. It came out like an apology. 'Different generation, different pressures. When we were young—well, when *I* was—life was structured, career-based. That was the king-pin. Hard slog, and then the big opportunity opened up. You followed where it led, all else disciplined to fit in: home, wife, family, leisure. The pattern: it took all our effort, attention, energy. Now they haven't any of that. No sure careers any more, just occasional jobs. No structure, you see. Only disappointments, rejections, their own whims to lead them. *Unsuccessful.* They haven't carapace enough to be safe left wandering in the world of ambition we created.'

His head sunk between hunched shoulders. Angus removed the empty glass from his fingers and went back to the bar. All he'd heard and seen served to confirm what the barman had told him, how Foden had first come to Crete in search of his runaway son. Judging by the way he had spoken of the young ones dying, one must suppose he'd lost hope. And so drank. All the same, Angus thought, the advent of Miles had had some little effect. There remained a chance that Foden was not actually flotsam himself but the decrepit beachcomber who'd learned to value it.

When he returned to their table Angus carried two large filter coffees, double strength. He put one down in front of Foden. 'Get this inside you. We need to talk. Because I need your help.'

He waited until the other had complied and was eyeing him warily, then he told him what Miles's arrival had interrupted, about himself and Paula, right from the beginning at Heathrow, ending with the brush-off at Security Police headquarters that day.

'Could you—' Foden sounded dubious, scanning his face, 'Could you repeat the whole interview word for word?'

'I'll try. It went this way . . .'

As Foden listened he was at first anxious, then he seemed to relax. The beginnings of a bleak smile showed. 'Sweet music to my ears,' he murmured. 'Your Kápetan's one of my own kind, talks like a Civil Servant. Our language is the same, it seems, all the world over.'

'Saying nothing with a lot of verbiage,' Angus ground out.

'Not at all. You're prejudiced. It wasn't what you wanted to hear. I don't think you really listened to him.'

'Good God, man, he was saying he didn't want to know!'

Foden shook his head wisely. 'Wrong! He was saying he didn't want *you* to know what *he* knew, but he did want to know of anything you might pick up. Think back. Or do I have to translate?'

'He was stone-walling, no more.'

'To some extent, but leaving a good gap in the wall at one point. He didn't warn you off, did he? They don't hesitate to pack your bags and put you on the plane if they're really clamping down. No, he dressed up official policy, then let you see that theory wasn't identical with practice. They don't want *interference*, but admit that in your case you're a policeman too and can't keep yourself from poking around. Correct so far?'

'Well, that's one way of reading what he said.'

'Then he restated the facts of the case as officially recorded: that Paula had left the country as planned. And let you counter with your suspicions, as yet unconfirmed by any document, that identities had been switched. Challenging you to get busy on that end, don't you see? He must get it officially referred from Frankfurt or London before he can get things moving here. Investigations have to be sanctioned and budgeted for. And then finally you hinted at conspiracy to cover an immigration offence. Pointing the finger! Oh, he's on the job all right. You can risk good money that the wires were humming and the Security system pulsating before ever you'd turned the corner of the street.'

'I'd like to believe you. But why the hell can't he come out and say as much openly?'

'It isn't the way it's done here,' Foden said sadly. 'If you make a nuisance of yourself they temporize until you get tired and go away. Not so long back, when the Colonels were in power, they tried being more direct, and look where it got them. The police have a reputation, possibly merited in some cases, that makes treble choirboys of the PLO and KGB by comparison.'

'But I won't get tired, and I won't go away.'

'They're counting on it in your case, believe me. Anything you do now, they'll be just one step behind all the way. Get right to the end of the trail and it's there they'll trip you, for the pleasure of getting in first. Which, as you're so anxious to find your girl, you should be grateful for, unless, of course . . .'

'Unless what?'

Foden looked nervously away. His face was strained. 'Unless they're actively involved themselves. In which case everything's stacked against you. The chances of reaching the end of the trail would be nil.'

'The police involved in Paula's disappearance? What could she have done to upset them? She thinks before she acts. She was on holiday.'

Foden hesitated before he answered. 'That's only half the situation,' he said gently. 'Her going missing, I mean. There's the other half to consider: somebody getting out of the country in her place. Suppose that was the angle your Kápetan came in on. Suppose he owed someone a big favour, someone in need of concealment.' Foden's lips tightened. 'Who would have been in the best position to demand an alien's passport and effect a switch?'

Angus sat motionless and dumb. It wasn't an entirely new thought. Wasn't that what had been lurking in the recesses of his mind, forbidden to come forward into the light? Paula efficiently, professionally, done away with, so that she could never tell the truth of any cover-up. A statistic of police brutality. No, even in Greece there couldn't be irony like that.

Foden stretched slowly, stood up, emptied a handful of loose change on the table. His face was lifeless. 'You could go and ask your Kápetan again about Paula Musto, the girl he hadn't heard of. Ask him particularly about the night of August tenth. He took her statement himself.'

'About what? What happened?' Angus was transfixed.

Foden rasped a hand across his chin and gazed over the sunlit terrace and the street beyond. He let an accelerating motorbike dash noisily past drawing a trailer piled with vegetables, before he spoke again. 'A small boy fell off the hotel roof. It's in their files. Paula was down below. Probably information quite useless for your purpose, but it could do no harm to pursue it. Shake the Kápetan's complacency a little?'

'Thanks. I'll get on it right away.'

*

When Mott arrived for the second time at the police post he was surprised to be shown in almost at once. Perhaps they had more information on him by now. Three large uniformed men who seemed to fill the small office rose from their seats, stared hard at him and nodded as they left. The Kápetan waved a hand, not in greeting but to disperse tobacco smoke. 'Detective-Inspector Mott,' he addressed him correctly.

'Mr will do quite nicely.'

'Mr Mott, please take a chair. You have news for us?'

'Nothing progressive.' He faced the Greek policeman squarely. 'Retrospective—August tenth, late evening. I understand a child was killed falling from a hotel roof. Not a thing to happen often?'

'Probably unique. I remember it well. Not so much late evening as almost midnight. The case is of interest to you?'

'Paula Musto made a statement, witness after the event.'

'This is the lady you are inquiring about?'

'You know damn well it is.'

The Kápetan considered him. He had not moved from his chair at the desk where he slouched, arms negligently spread over his papers. On an instant he changed. The eyes hardened, he sat straight, nodded briskly. 'Sit down, Mr Mott. You shall see the case notes.'

He reached into his top drawer and pushed across to the Englishman a file he had ready. 'I do not think you read our language, but there is an English summary on top. The originals of most statements are in English too. The rest have translations. I will leave you with them. Please make yourself comfortable.'

From another drawer he produced a pad of lined paper. This and a ceramic jug crammed with ballpoint pens he placed beside the file. Then he heaved himself to his feet. 'I am obliged to go out now, but my assistant is next door. He is instructed to help in every way.' So saying, he gave a derisory bow, lifted a pair of field glasses from the crowded windowsill and went out.

'*Au revoir, Kápetan.*'

So, he had been expected, and provision made for his reception. Mott didn't care for this cat-and-mouse attitude. Or was it the playground game of Grandmother's Footsteps? No doubt the file was suitably sanitized to keep him off the track, or even spiced with red herring? God, all he wanted was to find Paula, and to find her fast. Damn them for devious tricksters. What were they afraid of? He'd no intention of finding fault or reviewing relative police methods.

He pulled a ballpoint from the bunch on offer. The jar they stood in depicted, classically, the Labours of Hercules. As well it might.

The inquiry was detailed, as far as it went. The Kápetan's assistant, who weightwise played Goebbels to his Goering, answered his queries readily. Yes, they were satisfied that the statements made were mainly true. Even the boy Van Leiden's? Yes, well, since the second had contradicted the first, only one could be believed. Which? The man shrugged. Where was the boy now? In Athens, with his mother, at another hotel. The address was here. And the Italian gentleman who escorted Miss Musto that evening? His home address was Rome, but in filming one was a bird of passage.

Mott wrote down the two addresses, tight-lipped. 'If the boy lied, why leave it here?' he pursued.

'His second statement, refuting the first, agrees with facts as stated by the other witnesses,' the little dried-up man explained legalistically. 'It rounds off the file. In the eyes of our superiors.'

Mott looked up, sensing there was more to come. He wasn't disappointed. Quite suddenly the man smiled, and was transformed. He laid down a clip of papers he had brought in with him. 'So we opened a second file, to go a little further. I have added English translations for you, but briefly it stands like this. In his first statement the boy Desmond claimed he heard two people arguing. He identified them as the Egyptian film-girl and her Arab admirer. Both deny being on the roof and have witnesses to their alibis. But the roof garden was dark in places and the boy could have been mistaken in what he thought he saw. Yet he *heard* an argument, at the end of which the man swore in Arabic. Using words the boy was able to repeat. He had spent several months in Tangier with his mother, and first heard them there.'

'Two *other* people?'

'It seems possible. Two persons of similar description who might need to hold a private meeting there, having no alternative venue. One, male or female, perhaps staying in the hotel, who shares a bedroom and so lacks privacy. There is no Arab man who fits those circumstances, so him we look for elsewhere, in the list of such persons known to be at present on Crete. It is necessary, you understand, to keep such matters documented for security reasons. On this we ask your discretion.'

'Thank you.' Mott took the paper and ran his eye down the two lists of names. Some had been underlined. Others had a cross against them and a word in Greek. 'What does this mean?' Mott pointed.

'Eliminated. After investigation.'

'You are continuing to go through the others?'

'Go through?' The man was uncertain of the idiom's precise meaning.

'You intend to continue investigating them?'

'This case is not closed. Very open, in fact.'

'And in your opinion there could be a connection between this Sayid's death and Paula's disappearance?'

'The same hotel; Miss Musto a near-witness. Loose—if a connection at all—but we cannot overlook it. You may have more success yourself, Mr Mott, among those who knew her. A tourist among tourists. Gossip. *Tittle-tattle*, isn't it?'

It was too slow a method. Time could be what Paula hadn't a lot of. It could already have run out. But there was no other angle for him to come in on.

The visitors were beginning to disperse, who had been here during Paula's week on Crete. He must keep on at Foden who'd led him this far, find out if he'd noticed who she spent most time with. He looked again down the list of Arabs. 'Anything promising here?'

The Kápetan's assistant hesitated. Then he put a finger against a name. 'Hard drugs from Turkey, Bulgaria. We leave him to swim, then we catch the big fish later.' His finger moved on. 'This one, Libyan, very dangerous. We watch him very carefully because he watches others. Sometimes they disappear. We think they go by sea. Perhaps by *caïque*. Or else into it, weighted.'

He crackled the paper. 'And this one becomes interesting. Ex-PLO, we think. His second visit, illegal entry from the south. So he too could be Libyan-based, a trainee terrorist, even a graduate making contact with unknown persons here. The others, probably clean. Or only—gritty? No, *grubby*. Merchants mostly. Of this and that.'

'Any slave trade?' Angus asked stiffly.

Again there was a slight hesitation. 'Girls? We have wondered. That would be something new for Crete. But the coming of tourists in great numbers changes things. A different financial climate, the money vultures gather. But mostly it would be cabaret girls from the mainland, girls trained to please, that they are interested in, not—fresh ones.'

Mott kept his head down. 'Thanks. I'll go on digging.'

The visit was over. He wished he didn't feel that somewhere he'd passed over an important point.

He rose and offered the man his hand, mollified that now he was at least allowed to trail a few stages behind the official investigation.

The phone rang. As he prepared to leave, the man signalled him to wait. When he replaced the receiver his expression was sombre. 'I am to arrange a car for you. It seems that a body has been found, a woman's. The Kápetan requires you to go with him to see it.'

It took only a few minutes to the Old Harbour. Angus recognized the grim Venetian fortress as they flashed by, then they were among fishing-boats and the air was strong with diesel fumes. The little crowd of rubbernecks consisted entirely of visitors. Only a nod from the uniformed men on duty was needed to keep the locals away. The Kápetan was talking with two swarthy men in oily sweaters. When he saw Angus he waited, then nodded him for'ard where the nets lay all among the gear. With the body still caught up in them.

'It will be difficult,' the Kápetan warned. 'Several days in the water, Spiro thinks, and he has experience in these matters. There is oily deposit, because it was tied down among the boats, but that has served at least to keep the fish off.'

'Let's get it done, then.' Angus moved up, crossed the gang-plank and looked down at a bundle of indeterminate limbs and soiled rags. He turned away momentarily, focused on the skyline and looked back. He forced himself to drop down into the body of the boat.

'There,' said the Kápetan unnecessarily.

Hard-eyed, Angus went close. He bent down over her. The body must have floated on its back, because the face was almost intact, with areas quite free of the black grease.

'Do you recognize the woman?'

Angus drew a deep breath. 'Yes.'

CHAPTER 15

For a moment there was no sound at all. A momentary paralysis of the brain, Angus thought afterwards. It was like a break in a recording, an instant of nothing, and then he was extra aware of the noises restored: the low chug of small engines, the suck and cloop of water between hull and harbour wall, a cry of gulls, a murmur of voices, grit under someone's shoe, the high-pitched strumming of halyards against aluminium masts. And his own voice echoing. 'Yes,' he said again, to dispel the sound of it the first time.

He moved his weight on to one foot. 'I'm almost certain.' He reached in the breast pocket of his shirt for the wallet of photographs, looked through until he found the one he wanted. 'There. I think that's the one.' He willed his voice to stay flat, although he was exultant. Not Paula, thank God. Anyone else but Paula. Foden had told him these were the two Belgian nurses.

'Irène Petitjean,' he said.

'Ah.' Evidently the Kápetan knew of her. 'The older of the Belgian women,' he added.

'In which case,' Angus demanded, 'where's the other, Sylvie Audoin?' His eyes met those of the Kápetan who nodded slowly, and he answered himself in a flat undertone, 'Gone back home, on Paula's passport?'

The Kápetan went into action, dispatching minions in all directions. Not entirely a show put on for the onlookers' benefit, Angus observed wryly, but there was a strong element of theatre in the procedure. When he had a space cleared about him he saw fit to remember that the English policeman was still there. 'Mr Mott, I will have the car take you back to your hotel.'

'I can walk, thank you.'

'As you wish. We are grateful for the identification. Happy too that it is not, as feared, the body of your friend.'

'You didn't need me to identify a woman I'd never met. Weren't your own photographs good enough?'

'Ours? You think that the dead woman is a known criminal?'

'I mean that your police cameraman was busy enough last Monday with a telephoto lens from the building behind the hotel. Paula wasn't the only guest sunning herself on her balcony. I think you have Irène Petitjean too in your album.'

If a giant toad could look impish then that was the Kápetan's expression then. 'You are clever, Mr Mott. And you guess correctly. I too was able to identify the body, from a photograph. As I told you before, we take precautions over our visitors.'

'May I ask how the woman died?'

'I ask myself the same thing. Our medical experts will shortly do their best to give an answer. Perhaps if you telephone me at this hour tomorrow—?'

He was giving nothing away. Mott had a strong intuition that he'd get farther himself on a loose rein. Drily he thanked the Kápetan and took his leave, turning back to 25th August Street. By the time he reached the hotel on foot two police cars were already parked at the kerb beyond the terrace. From his balcony he could actually hear the Kápetan's voice with another's. The men were standing directly below him. So that would be the room the two nurses shared. And when Paula thought she was being photographed, the real subject was maybe one floor down. Horizontal direction was easier to pinpoint than elevation from a distance. He must take a closer look at Paula's last two frames.

He stood silent, listening, and suddenly Andy Whitelaw's voice came clearly up to him. 'But how d'you tie it in with the other business?'

'She wore pyjamas to sleep in,' said the Kápetan in English.

How's that for a *non sequitur*, Angus asked himself. What had pyjamas to do with the case? Apparently nothing if 'the other business' was Paula's disappearance. If, however, they were discussing the boy's fall off the roof—yes, there had been something in Des's first statement. He had recognized the Arab by his language, and the girl by her harem pants glimpsed when she passed the floodlight. The difference between those and flared pyjamas would be in the ankle shaping, and that level would be below the source of light fixed on the low inner coping. What Des had seen was the Petitjean woman in secret discussion with an unknown Arab. He, or she, or both, had discovered the second small eavesdropper and made short work of him. Now Irène herself was dead. Had the man found it necessary to silence her too?

The Kápetan had reached this point in the reasoning earlier, before Angus made his guess at who the dead woman was, and that was why he hadn't been at all astonished, although she was supposed to be on a mini-cruise now with the Hungarians.

But at least she had come back to Iraklion. Could he assume that Paula had done so too? He needed more information, and must keep on at the Fiesta crowd.

The restaurant was fast filling with diners, and although not hungry he let himself be waved across to the double table, determined to get his money's worth in information: this time a thorough interrogation of who actually saw the party return from Mátala on Tuesday evening.

The New Zealand couple had come on Irène at Reception as she picked up her key, and the car was at the kerb as they went out. That meant, probably, that Paula had just gone up, and the Hungarians had previously been dropped off in town to change for dinner.

Irène had said what a marvellous day it had been. They'd

picnicked on an island, and that had given Frau Toller the idea for a mini-cruise including Santorini and Lindos on Rhodes. They'd come back to drop off Paula and get fresh clothes, and were off that night, all four. Mrs Scott quite envied them their good fortune.

So the next question was—did they go? And if Irène's body was found by a boatman near Iraklion harbour, had there been some disaster involving both nurses and the Hungarian couple? As Mrs Scott had now told all this to the Kápetan he would be checking on charter boats large enough for sea-going expeditions, and applying for authority to look inside Frau Toller's rented apartment in town.

There was no part for Angus in all this. The only thing left to him was to walk the city streets among the Saturday night crowds, as Paula must have done a week ago, and await the Kápetan's pleasure to learn if anything new had come to light.

A new harbour scene overlaid the grimmer one etched on his mind. It was gay now with coloured lights and beflagged small craft bobbing on the water. There were parties on board and parties in the crowded *tavernas* ashore. In a half-lit angle between two alleys a group of sad clowns were miming, dancing in silence with white-painted faces. He thought of the lost ones the big waiter had spoken of. Perhaps these were some of them, on the same wasteful route as Foden's dead son.

He looked for the retired Civil Servant, but he was not to be found. Dissatisfied and apprehensive, Angus went back to the hotel, borrowed some trunks from Colonel Martin and swam hard for twenty minutes up and down the pool until tired enough for bed. He awoke next morning to a bright room and a restless need for action.

Beneath his deadweight anxiety for Paula was the professional response, the need for system in his search but, frustratingly, no routine available to hang it on, no normal links to use for the established Missing Person procedure.

And then Crete itself, so defiantly different, forcing him at the same time to be right outside, a foreigner, a *tourist* for God's sake! Not even having the language to ask his questions in.

He was dismayed at his own impotence and the muddle of it all, just as Crete itself was a muddle, superficially emerging so fast into the modern world while its ancient glories flaked and crumbled imperceptibly away, succeeding epochs picking over the rubble of earlier ages for materials to press into practical use, and in this way disturbing the strata of time.

He was moved by a metaphysical sense quite alien to him, that Paula was there in much the same way, covered over by shifting débris, a casualty of others' actions, weakly alive and waiting.

The experience had been strongest when he awoke, conscious that he'd been dreaming of her, although the precise memory eluded him. There remained a warmth, an undeserved peace almost instantly lost when the reality of his predicament returned. His smouldering anger increasingly demanded some object to wreak itself upon. And the wildly beautiful island lay unchanged under the unrelenting sun, not giving a thing away, mocking him.

The people—the Cretans themselves—seemed equally unmoved. Civil, watchful, alert. And apart. He couldn't reach them, didn't even know that he needed to. Paula wasn't one of them. The clue to her puzzle should lie among those she was closest to: either the group from Fiesta who'd travelled from Athens with her and were still here for their second week, or those who'd returned on the flight she should have taken back. Why the hell hadn't Frankfurt come up yet with something on the girl who'd taken her place? She couldn't have disappeared into thin air. Could he even be sure that the Kápetan was inquiring of the Belgian authorities whether Sylvie Audoin had been sighted near home?

Try another angle. If someone had substituted for Paula *in Iraklion,* then Paula was still here, in some state. He had to face it, say it out loud to himself: Paula still here, dead or alive.

Right, then. So the other girl had left a gap. Was Paula filling it? A straightforward switch? Not willingly on Paula's part, he knew. She wouldn't have ditched him without apology or explanation. She had too much courtesy at least, wouldn't ruin the once-a-year holiday plans of others like Barry and Angie, hanging on for her at Chichester harbour.

So, back to seeing her as a casualty of someone else's machinations. Follow up the girl who ought still to be here and wasn't, the girl on the plane. Wispy light hair under the wig, Kate Drummond had said. Not all Greeks were dark, even here on Crete, so she could have been a local. But much more likely a foreigner who could book out and disappear without causing comment. And taking Paula's luggage. So where was her own?

He chased up the chambermaid who looked after the third-floor section, and learned that the Belgians' luggage was still in their room. As it would be, whether Sylvie was yet to be brought out of the sea like Irène, or was the impostor on Paula's flight.

Why should Sylvie Audoin assume anyone else's identity? Either because she was afraid and in hiding, or she had to cover up Paula's disappearance. Both alternatives had strong criminal implications. There was an even more sinister possibility: she was running to escape a charge of murder. It wasn't yet known how the older nurse had died. If there had been violence, wasn't the instigator more likely to be the unknown Arab?

But could there in fact have been a simple sailing accident? With Irène Petitjean drowned, must the others be too— Frau Toller, her son, and Paula?

This morning Angus found Foden at the first place he

looked, in his accustomed sun-spot at a table in Eleftherías Square. He looked markedly different, more careworn, sitting crouched instead of languidly outstretched. The drink in front of him had not been disturbed. 'I hoped you'd come,' he said, squinting up. 'I've been talking to a girl from the south. She was up here overnight, for supplies.'

Angus nodded, sliding on to a chair beside him. 'I suppose you heard about the body brought in by a boatman?'

'The nurse, yes. That's who I was asking about. She drove a party down to Mátala last Tuesday. Kanski, his mother and your girl Paula.'

'I know about that.'

'But this girl—this ragbag of a relic—said she tried to beg a lift to Iraklion on Petitjean's return journey, but the lady turned her down, and her passenger—an Arab girl— actually laid hands on her, pushed her into a ditch.'

'Where was this?'

'Midway between Mátala and Phaestos, on the way back. It happened about two o'clock. Driving through the siesta, quite mad.'

Angus sat frowning. 'So early, it could have been a diversionary trip. She could have gone back for the others later.'

'Perhaps. Perhaps not.'

The waiter had come for an order. 'What's that?' Angus demanded, pointing to Foden's drink.

'Oh, I'm fine, thanks.' The older man seemed confused. 'Nothing more.'

'Apple juice,' the waiter said obligingly, and Foden coloured.

'I'll take an *espresso*,' Angus told the waiter. He looked at Foden.

'Thought I'd bring the grey cells to bear without . . . *without*,' he excused himself.

'So what do they tell you?'

'I think—maybe—we should go to Mátala. Ask around.'

'We've too many women now,' Angus reflected. 'Where did the Arab girl spring from?'

'Like Aphrodite. Out of the sea. Wasn't there an Arab *man* too many last week? The one Des overheard on the roof. I think that boy was very lucky he left when he did. A pity the other little fellow didn't make off too.'

'They were up there together, you think?'

'At the same time, but the little one trailing Des. He used to do that. Des probably didn't know. He noticed the couple and faded. But Sayid, who was a prying pest at times, stayed on to listen.'

'What could they be discussing that necessitated killing an eavesdropper?'

'A matter of life and death. Risk to themselves. I think the answer is down at Mátala, because that's where the others failed to return from. It needn't have been Paula who used her bed that last night. Sylvie Audoin could have done that, if Petitjean had actually left as she said she was to do.'

'Petitjean talked about a picnic on an island, but at two in the afternoon she was already on her way home,' Angus reconsidered.

'Leaving the others stranded. Literally, on some uninhabited coast?'

'You're right. We have to go and find out. Where can I hire a reliable car?'

'No problem. Kostas will take us. I always use him. He comes from Mátala too. His family is there. He has a six-year-old Citröen, the pride of his life, and he's steady as they come. A professional chauffeur, but he helps out sometimes in the Maze Bar.'

'The gorilla?'

Foden shrugged. 'Your Paula called him a bear. He's the original Gentle Giant. But useful if there's a rough-house. I gave him a call. He's standing by in case we need him.'

Angus narrowed his eyes and considered. 'I don't believe Petitjean's story of preparing for a cruise to Santorini. She made it up to account for the absences, and because she already had the picnic boat trip on her mind. In any case, if Frau Toller did suddenly arrange something of the sort, it could only have been during that day at Mátala. And she would have booked the trip there. So Mátala it is. Drink up your apple juice. We're on our way.'

There were brief moments on the journey when Angus almost forgot what it was all for, so breathtaking were the mountains towering above and then the valleys opening below. As they climbed by hairpin bends Angus leaned out and thrilled to the sight of a hawk planing in a rocky gorge below. It made an eagle of him.

Kostas, at first as dour and rugged as the upper crags, humanized as they dropped to the Messara Plain—so lush that grass reached up to the lowest branches of the olive trees. With distended nostrils he breathed in the resinous scent of pines, and in every small village its mixture of woodsmoke, stewing lamb and aromatic herbs. He started to talk—about his family; his sceptical acceptance of the new consumer luxuries; his problems with neighbours who flocked in friendly enthusiasm to his TV and would not leave at night to let him and Ariadni go to bed. At last, in desperation, he had started to undress in front of them, so now he was branded as an immoral man.

'You could have taken out your teeth and put them in a tumbler,' Angus said, remembering his grandfather's dismissal of late stayers.

'They are all my own. Besides—you do not know our village. They would have passed them round, tried them in. They are very friendly people.'

'Kostas has doubts about the island picnic,' Foden ventured.

'The coast is a pig,' Kostas said, 'especially for little boats. Only Mátala is good, until Mirtos, nearly at Ierápetra. And squalls come from the mountains, very dangerous. You need a good boat, a very good man for it. My brother will say.'

So it came down to that, Angus considered. Perhaps a storm at sea. Irène might have told them what happened, at least where to start looking, but she was dead. One thing was certain now. She had not been one of the Tuesday boat party. No way could any storm have blown her body from the Libyan Sea more than two hundred miles up a twisting coastline to Iraklion harbour.

He watched the laboriously cultivated plain roll by. Here inland every square metre of soil was used, mainly for olives, oranges, vines, carobs and almonds, as well as vegetables. From above, the land was a chequerboard regularly polka-dotted with olive trees, webbed with vines, and terraced up to the near-vertical. As they drove farther south the two mountain masses of the Dikti and Ida fell back from open, baked earth; heat bored into them and danced in mirages on the metalled road ahead. After seventy kilometres they came on Mátala suddenly. The end of a glaring, sandy road where the square, white and ochre houses cast purple shadows. And between them lay the dazzling, turquoise sea.

To the left the town straggled off in a mixture of old houses with flaking stucco and more modern intrusions. Everywhere that tables and chairs could be crammed they were fitted in to make some semblance of a taverna. The gritty beach, strewn with barely clad sunbathers, curved away on the right to a weathered sandstone promontory which, honeycombed with square-mouthed caves, jutted into the sea like a gargantuan golden bank of TV screens set up higgledy-piggledy for the townsfolk opposite to monitor. Over the openings swarmed the brown bodies of swimmers who climbed up to explore the neolithic tombs, more recently the homes of hippy communes until the authorities' hygiene requirements forced them out and farther inland.

Stiffly Angus, Foden and Kostas climbed from the car, eased their shirts loose and looked for a place with drinks. From the flat roof of a nearby house a girl called down the old hippy greeting, 'Where y'from?' but Foden just waved

languidly and turned away. About twenty young people up
there, in swimsuits, healthy and tanned, weren't hippies but
the fantasizers who came after, collecting myths.

Foden led Angus to a bar near the beach, where they sat
drinking chilled wine until Kostas came back with his
sister-in-law, a little brown walnut of a woman with
currant-black eyes. She was embarrassed to be in such a
place at such a time. She should have been hard at work.
Tavernas, like siestas, were for the men.

She told them that Spiros had gone off yesterday to the
Saturday market at Mires and had stayed over. Perhaps she
could be of use in his place. She had not noticed the visitors
Kostas had asked about, but then there were so many in
the summer. As for the boats, they came and went all the
time, but one fisherman—Damon Skoufas—had been gone
for several days now. Difficult to say how long, because he
was a surly man and lived alone, outside the town; but his
house was empty and his mooring free from last Monday
night.

'A day too early,' Foden said.

'Unless he went elsewhere to pick them up, or get supplies.
What is he like?'

'He drink too much,' the woman said scornfully, 'as some
men do. And he do anything for money. Sell his sister, but
he has none. I cross the road if he come.'

'And the boat?'

'A caïque, like my husband's, but not good. The sails new
two years back, but the engine—perf!—dirty, like the man.'

'And the weather,' Kostas said sadly, 'I have to tell you
—bad. It come down Tuesday from the mountains, a white
demon. The morning very calm, then it strike. It do that
sometimes here.'

They discussed together where the boat might have
headed. There were the Nisídhes Paximádhia, two islets just
eight kilometres off shore, without shelter or anchorage. If
a boat broke up there, someone would have found wreckage

by now. So Skoufas had ventured out farther, perhaps towards Gávdhos or Gavdhopoúla. The notorious squalls from the gorges being northerly, a boat out in the open sea would have found it hard to make land again. Their best hope would be Órmos Kalón Liménon to the east. There was Mavronísi, a steep black rock barely eleven metres above sea level in the bay, but also smaller ones out of sight of land which sailors avoided because of their danger. As a boy Kostas had landed on some of them, but without his father's knowledge. If there was a hope of finding the lost people he would try it now, perform a sweep. If they were in luck, then his brother could make the salvage claim on Skoufas's caïque.

The sister-in-law loaded them with food, fruit, wine and coffee in a Thermos flask which was her newest proud possession. Angus helped Kostas check over the boat and fill the tank with diesel. The big Greek clucked approvingly as he heard the engine turning over. 'Good sailors,' he said proudly, 'all my family.'

It was almost a quarter to two as they slid away, using the engine to clear the shore, then making way under sail. They had spare fuel stowed but had no idea how far they must go. Kostas looked back anxiously towards the far mountain tops. The forecast was for fine weather, moderate to fresh winds, but here the forecasts could easily be wrong.

Angus called to Foden and asked for the hand compass. 'Not Foden,' said the man. 'I call you Angus. I'm Keith.'

Keith. Keith and Kostas. Ridiculous how that K kept turning up to confound him. '*Goodbye drinks at K's*,' Angus said aloud.

Foden raised his head and asked him to repeat it. Then Angus explained about the final diary entry, and how he'd tried to work out what Paula had planned for her last night on Crete.

Foden gave his lopsided smile. 'It wasn't a date with me, more's the pity. How about you, Kostas? She did frequent the bar sometimes when you were on duty.'

'*Maze* Bar,' Kostas said huffily. 'Not *K*'s bar.'

'Maybe it's not important,' Angus granted. 'It was an appointment never kept, after all.' He stayed silent listening as water hissed past the hull, creaming and foaming into a curving wake. The sails tightened without a hint of slack.

'No clouds yet,' Kostas said. 'Pray God it stay so.'

Foden was shivering in the full glare of the sun. He took out a hip flask and drank, not offering it to the others. He did not like the sea.

Pray God a lot of things, Angus thought fervently: that Skoufas's old tub had reached land and they were all alive, able to hang on a little longer. And, given all that, that we're heading in the right direction now.

CHAPTER 16

Skoufas was a tough old ruffian but he was afraid now. He should not have played the fox so long, tinkering with the engine and pretending that something wasn't quite right. But the woman whom Zeid Khalida had sent to pick up the Libyan girl had insisted on no return tonight. She had paid him well for the delay, in drachmas hidden now under the floor of his house, and in *ouzo*. Perhaps if he hadn't drunk so deeply of it he wouldn't feel so queer now, unable to force the old boat's blunt nose round in the squally wind. Strange, because he was well used to drink and it had never done this to him before. However hard he tried to hold her the caïque was driving sideways on, rolling abominably, the engine ragged and inclined to splutter.

He should have stuck to what he'd arranged with the Khalida woman. It was the young man's fault that he'd changed the plan, offering him even more to get them back on shore, anxious because the girl had a plane to catch from

Iraklion tomorrow. Safer to have stayed where they were, on Gavdhopoúla, and the old woman, the mother, had seemed secretly pleased that they were stranded; but the money had spoken loudest. Even feeling as he did—head reeling and hands uncertain—he had pushed out the boat to go back to the mainland.

Already it was dangerously late, because clouds had built up on the far peaks, and suddenly the unnatural stillness was cracked open as the demon squealed down the gorges and whipped up heaving mountains and valleys in the sea itself. Through blinding spray the land seemed farther off, disappeared.

He knew then that they would never make Mátala; with luck perhaps some eastern point of the southern coast. If the engine held out. Impossible to use any sail. He'd barely got them lashed before the fury hit. They would have been ripped to rags, the masts shattered, the old tub driven farther south, out adrift in the Libyan Sea. So he'd only the engine, and although there was diesel enough for the normal return journey, with the storm to fight he was burning it all just to hold his position. The time would come when—

He was old, and unbelievably tired. Never before had it taken so much out of him to wrestle with the tiller. His head was falling on his chest and his hands had no more strength than a baby's. The old woman came astern and shouted through the wind but he could not grasp the words, the world of sea was spinning about him as he fell.

She hauled him off the tiller and he went down on the boards, sliding until his head lay by her knees, propped against the boat's timbers. And she was trying to hold the course, an old woman like her, while he slipped down into the dark.

Paula too had her hands full. She had seen Jozsef fumbling for his tablets and was prepared when the fit came on him. It was more severe than that time in the lift. She straightened him out on the boards, but water slopped all around and more kept sleeting in to drench them with every plunge the boat took into a trough. She needed to get across to Magda, who seemed to know what she was about but didn't have the strength to hang on indefinitely against such a force of wind and sea.

'Rocks!' Magda shouted. 'Hold on. Save Jozsef!' She was lurching and the engine choked. Ahead, low through the heaving water, Paula saw something black appear and disappear, and then come rushing at them.

They grounded with a terrible force that flung them for'ard. The bows shot high as the engine broke away aft. The timbers shrieked and burst apart. Water was pouring in, then it was water all around, and Paula was being alternately tossed like a cork and thrust down under a great weight, but her hands were tight on Jozsef's arms, supporting him as she tried to turn on her back.

For a moment her feet touched rock, but then she was swept on again, tumbled over and over, the man almost torn from her grasp. And incredibly Magda had reached them. They made a sort of raft, locked together, Jozsef still conscious but suffering terrible tremors. When the coma came it was easier for them. Only the battering of the sea then, and that was enough.

There had been no proper shore. They had swum round the rock to leeward and there, in comparative shelter, they'd clung on with bleeding fingers until Paula found strength to climb and heave Jozsef up while Magda supported him from below. Lastly the old woman was dragged out and they lay, still washed over by occasional waves, coughing out water like failing pumps. Sea and spray obscured their vision, and when at last the squall was past and they could look out, there was no sign at all of Skoufas or his boat.

The cave reminded Paula of the neolithic tomb at West Kennet. In fact it was smaller, a single chamber, a recess shaped like a dog's hind leg, halfway up the rockface and extended at some time by rocks piled together at the entrance, on the very edge of an overhang. She had found it accidentally, and it had taken hours getting the others up here. Inside it was dark and strangely cold, but dry. They had climbed up the opposite, easier side of the crag and then dropped down. Beneath, it was precipitous to the sea and black rocks. Now all three lay huddled together, sharing warmth, sleeping off their exhaustion, still in their drenched clothes.

When morning came and they took stock there was little to reassure them. To judge from the diffused brightness of the masked sun, their shelter faced roughly south-east. Help, if it came, would be from the other side of their rock. Their clothes were still damp and they had no food. More serious, Jozsef's drugs, which were his daily control, had gone down with the boat. They had to assume that Skoufas had drowned. He had been in no condition to save himself.

'We couldn't have done any more,' Paula told Magda, but the older woman required no reassurance, had no qualms of conscience.

'He might have been washed up on the other side,' the girl said. 'I'm going to climb up again and go over the top. We must find food, and some way of signalling to passing ships.'

She came back when the sun had burnt its way through sullen cloud and was high overhead. She wore only her black top, a white waist slip and a pair of briefs. The tatters of her orange skirt were weighted down with stones on the rockface facing the mainland. Its bright colour was all she had to signal with. There was no sight of land, no Skoufas, no food but a doubtful clump of rooty plants and a tuft or two of dried-up grass. They were in the Ancient Mariner's situation: thirsty and surrounded by water, none of it drinkable.

'I am thinking,' said Magda regretfully, 'of all that food left over, which we didn't want yesterday.'

Paula watched her with fascinated curiosity. Yesterday when, through incompetence, Skoufas could have stranded them overnight on Gavdhopoúla, she was angry. Because of Jozsef's distress on her account she'd made no complaint, but she hadn't missed Magda's evident satisfaction. And when, immediate upon Jozsef's bribing the boatman, the engine had been declared in order again, Paula's suspicions were confirmed. But the only explanation for Magda's inducing the man to strand them would be to prevent her own return to England and to keep her longer in their company.

In Jozsef's company, was that it? Surely Magda hadn't now cast her, Paula, in the role of desirable daughter-in-law? It was ludicrous, unthinkable. Yet that was a possibility she must consider.

Magda had been so brave in the storm, poor woman, the indomitable survivor who insisted that those she swept along with her should be survivors too. An exasperating, admirable old woman, for whom Paula must admit to a kind of pity. Now, when disaster was so wholesale, was no time for recrimination. 'Help will come,' Paula promised her, but had to admit to herself that it was taking its time arriving; and that evening just before sundown Jozsef went into an alarming series of attacks, the tremors and the coma alternating without any interval between. Eventually fatigue must have overcome the brain's frantic activity and he seemed to sleep.

Magda had taken off her own skirt and rolled it for a pillow under his head as he lay in the cave's far end. 'You must sleep too, Paula,' she insisted. 'Stay by him. I will sit at the opening. I do not sleep for long at night. Perhaps I shall see the lights of a passing ship.'

Paula thought it unlikely, and they had no means of making their presence known: no matches, no convenient Very lights, no magnifying lens, mirror or kindling. Only rock, which couldn't be eaten, ignited or made comfortable to lie on. All it did was tear the flesh of her fingers and her unshod left foot. She tried wearing her one sandal on each foot alternately and found that the stitching started to tear loose.

Jozsef continued to suffer the series of fits, each time more prolonged and distressing. She would not have believed that withdrawal of his drugs could have had such a terrible effect. He seemed to fail even as she watched him.

On the third day she came back to find Magda sitting in her customary place with a strange smile on her face. She behaved as though the cave and the inhospitable rock were the most normal place to be, as gracious as if she poured tea for friends from an antique silver service. It was the sun getting to her, Paula supposed, for the woman's face, like her own, was blistering, the lips so cracked that they bled. All the time there was the plaguing taste of salt.

When Paula went back to see to Jozsef he wasn't breathing. She thought Magda must surely know. In any case she had no intention of being the one to tell her. She took off her waist slip and laid it over Jozsef's face. Soon she would have no clothes at all.

That afternoon she went back to the north side of their rock, but there was no speck of life on the surface of the sea and no shade to be had. She thought at one point that she heard a distant plane but could see nothing. Her sight was becoming defective after staring into so much light. Objects a few feet from her began to have double outlines and dance about. She had stomach cramps, and when she'd eaten grass she threw it up a few minutes afterwards. She found she trembled, even in the sunlight.

Once when a stone seemed to move near her foot she discovered a tortoise. How it reached that bare rock and survived she could not guess. It looked old and shrivelled, but it was alive. She tried to think of it as meat, but she found it impossible. She rolled it away down the rocks where she could not ever be tempted to go after it, and it went too far, splashed into the sea.

Back at the cave Magda had started to talk in a low, monotonous voice, telling the terrible story of her life. Paula listened a while, then went back to her watching-post on the other side of the rock. Under the ledge she sat on there was a patch of long-stemmed grass, bleached and leaning from the sea wind. She pulled a piece and it broke brittly in her hands. Hay already. But grass was the wild form of corn, wasn't it? In these miserable seeds, if she blew the chaff off, there would be a crude form of flour. Protein. Food.

She rubbed the shrivelled ears of grass between her hands, picked out the precious grains and set them between her teeth. Mixing with her saliva they gave a taste of gluey mould. She remembered the fungus that attacked barley (or was it rye?). Ergot, a dangerous convulsant which had sent whole country communities fatally mad in parts of southern Europe. If grass was corn for one purpose, then it could well be for another, as host to poisonous parasites.

As she looked up at the relentless sky its beauty of blueness mocked her. Momentarily it seemed to swing like a wind-blown canopy above her and she lost balance, had to sink on her knees and hold tight to the knotted roots of the peach-coloured grasses. Oh God, it was madness whichever way she went—by heatstroke, starvation or poisoning. This was a choice only the super-rational should make. And she knew she was well adrift from that.

That evening they had an uncooked soup of seawater and grass stems thickened with the flour. It was still dangerously salty and had pasty lumps, but Magda pronounced it very good and asked for more. She insisted that Paula take the scrapings back to Jozsef for a second helping, and the girl sat there in the cave's dark end, beside the mound of his body, draining the rock bowl herself and running her fingers greedily round its rough inside to get the last lumpy dregs. And in the middle of swallowing she was retching at the foetid stench, terrified that the nourishment, poor as it was, would come gushing back and so be lost. But it stayed down and for a while the cramps lessened.

She looked dumbly at the broken face of her watch. She caught herself at it and realized that the action was triggered by the thought of time running out. And then she recognized something more—that she had given up hope. Before she ate she had wanted to draw life out forever. The survival instinct had driven her to eat, risking poison. Since then she had passed a frightful milepost. Her remaining hope was fixed on how soon it all might end.

Magda was getting crazier. She never went into the far end of the cave to visit Jozsef now nor asked about his condition. She alternated between a past when she was younger than Paula and some fictional projection in which Paula had joined her family, was presumably Jozsef's wife. She regarded the far end of the cave as out of bounds to herself since it was the young people's home and she wished to accord them privacy. She spoke of children, some-times meaning her own son, sometimes even herself. And again there was the forward projection which featured Paula.

'You will have children,' she said softly in her idiot sing-song voice. 'Yours and Jozsef's. I have always known that one day I should be a grandmama. You can have no idea how difficult it was having my little baby, running from Hungary as I did, spending days, nights, in hiding among the hills and woods. They kept watch all the time on the border, and there were hundreds more like me. Many were hunted down and taken back, or else shot in the attempt to get away. But I won, I got through to Austria.

'I would not let him be born there, you see. In Hungary. We had to cross first. I was no longer young, having my first child, and there was no safe place to rest up. He wanted so much to be born and I had to force him back. It was as though I was being born myself, unable to get through and refusing to go back.

'What wolves they were! I remembered when they first came, after the Germans. They called us Fascists, Nazi swine. They shot and raped and hanged anyone it pleased them to terrify. You do not forget that, ever. It stays in the mind for all time. Sometimes it seemed to grow so that your mind was nothing else but destruction and evil. I had to fight it, to remember that there were other things in life.

'That is how I stayed sane, how I kept a corner of my mind free of their bestiality. I remembered being a child myself at home, in the white and gold nursery, at play in the cool, shaded dairy, up on tiptoe to peer inside the great bowls brimming with creamy milk. There were bright tiles on the floor there and I remembered how my little leather shoes rang out on them and their echo came back at me off the painted walls.

'And sometimes I would pretend I was riding after my brothers again on my fat pony with the red leather saddle, or sitting on my grandfather's lap to play with his soft golden beard. A child left over from a world blown to pieces.

'But I knew that one day I would have a child of my own and he would go on. Go on and on. The children in the portraits on the stairs. So many of them, but all with my face, *our* face.'

She smiled and beckoned Paula closer as if to share a secret. 'My father's mother. She had the same face I have. My grandmama. And when I am a grandmother too, Jozsef's child will bear my face.'

'And I am to have his child?' Paula tried to humour her, but it was heartbreaking.

'Who else is there?' Magda's face darkened. 'I have been at my wits' end to find the right woman. He is—not strong. It was the manner of his being born that caused it. They said afterwards that there was damage. We thought at first he might not live.'

Her hands plunged about desperately, then she controlled them. The voice continued, deeper and with an underlying plea to be believed. 'He is a good man. There is no harm in him. There is nothing really wrong.'

Despite her own horror, Paula reached out a hand. 'All that is past. You're safe now, both of you.' She could barely suppress the tremor in her voice as she gave Magda the only comfort she could offer. 'And now I am with you.'

'Here, yes. With us. With him. And you will conceive his child. You are a good girl, Paula.'

Paula closed her eyes and willed herself not to think of the pathetic body in the cave's darkest corner, no longer stiff but discoloured in patches, noisy and swelling with gases. The stench was terrible but Magda seemed unaware. At some deep, deep level she must know he was dead, but her will would not permit it to be true.

'Go to him now,' the woman pleaded. 'It is evening and the light is almost gone. He needs you. I will stay here and guard the way in, so no harm can come. Good night, child. And say good night to him from me.'

She stretched herself across the opening of the cave, leaving no room to pass, and in stepping across there would be the choice of falling into space or bodily pushing her from the ledge. Paula dared take neither chance. Two corpses for company would double the horror, and she would be left utterly alone. The only option left was to crawl away into the darkness and lie down beside the dead thing that had lately been a shy, gentle young man.

She slept fitfully, dreaming several times in succession of waking and going about a confused version of her imprisoned life, so that each time she actually awoke she was not sure whether she still half-dreamt. Once or twice it seemed that someone else was there with the three of them, (Jozsef dead but still able to interrupt the others' conversation with whispered demands for attention.) It was as though the girl Magda had once been, who fought off the Russian invaders, had joined them. Paula leaned forward once to ask the girl's name and was told it, but on waking the name escaped her and this made her strangely uneasy. She began to think that the name was a clue to help them all find their way out of a maze.

Next day—or it may have been three or four days later, because she slept and awoke so many times, sometimes to dark and sometimes to light—there was the sound of rain. Paula could see that someone had been painting on the walls. There were the lovely flowing shapes of running deer and aurochs, and little stick men with spears and bows encircled them, like those in the caves of Lascaux. While she lay there watching the hunt—for the figures were all alive and active—a girl came and served her a savoury meal on a Lindos plate where the colours were the same as the cave walls—sand and ochre, terracotta and matt black, with touches of white like the tunic the girl wore.

It was the most delicious food Paula had ever tasted. She held the slippery cubes of meat in her fingers and the rich, spiced sauce ran down her chin and dripped on her wrists. But as she ate, in the recesses of her mind she knew pain, which grew in insistence until she was forced to let the dream slip. She awoke to darkness, gnawing hunger, and the cave's foetid stench.

There was no girl. There were no wall paintings, no food, no tiger brightness of light. But the background sound had been true. *It was raining.* She went out to the cave entrance and let water fill her mouth and hands, run down her arms. She piled small stones to make a sort of bowl and hoped it would hold the precious liquid. Between them she and Magda had nothing waterproof. She ran back and carefully unlaced Jozsef's shoes. There was nothing else. When the shower stopped she went back to her place and lay down exhausted.

She awoke to the sensation of being kissed. She felt the warm pressure of Angus heavy along her body which came alive at the touch. She reached her arms out. To nothing. To empty, foetid air. It was the cave again, the darkness and the stench of corruption. She listened for rain but there was no sound of it above the sighing of the sea and the soft lapping of water against the lower rocks. Even Magda was silent now. The low keening was over. Either she slept or she had passed into another phase of brooding withdrawal.

It would be evening or early morning. Whichever, it did not matter. Either the reflected light at the cave's mouth would brighten, hardening the pattern of the craggy walls, or it would fade away, as hope faded, even as hunger faded with time, leaving only a gnawing sickness, swimming vision, a curious procession of impossible spectres flowing fitfully through the mind.

But the light refused to dim. Slowly it penetrated farther into her den, reached out, making demands on her. And then Magda too started calling—a desperate, cracked appeal that she could not deny. While Magda survived she must as well. But not for too long. She must use herself up. To be left alive here alone was too terrible.

On hands and knees Paula crept towards the daylight. No, it was moonlight, bright and silver. She leaned swaying over the cliff's edge and looked down into the haze of rock and green sea. A bird cried out overhead, one of those dusty-magpie sort which were so common here.

She was hallucinating again, because briefly she thought she heard voices. They were men's, and not Greek. That was how she knew they couldn't be real; because they sounded English, although the words hadn't reached her. She remembered the television in her Fulham flat; switching on the news; Alastair Burnet—wasn't that his name?—reading it. No, two newscasters. They bounced the items between them, quietly, soberly, turning it into dialogue; and now she had managed to dream up the actual words. '. . . sitting in the stern with the wake streaming out behind, and all the time getting farther and farther away.'

That was sad, although it didn't make much sense to her, but the dream was becoming a good one. She'd lost the television people and it was Angus speaking now, his voice going on and on about water. Water, that she so much needed. Needed Angus, would give anything to see him once more, hold him hard against her.

Water streaming *away*, he'd said, but his voice was nearer now, coming clearer every second. Coming from—*above*?

She leaned in the cave opening, twisting to look up, and saw nearby the miracle of greenness. The rain, so soon past, had made some dormant seed burst open and it had started to grow. A thread of tender stem, with two tiny leaves curved like supplicating hands. She reached up and plucked it, brought it close to her pricking eyes.

It was a ball of green fluff torn from Magda's jacket. For all that, she put it on her tongue, tried to wet it enough to swallow it down.

And then she mistily realized what she should have known at once: that she had reached the cliff's edge unhindered. Magda was no longer there blocking the cave's entrance. So she had marvellously recovered and gone off to forage.

The seabird mewed again and was echoed immediately by the woman's voice, crying distantly from somewhere below. Paula leaned out over the vertiginous wavering of rocks and sea. The outlines of objects kept changing, flowing into one another, but if she centred her mind on the scene below she could see—or was it more delusion?—another patch of green some distance down, almost directly below. But there had been no path, no way at all to get there. If Magda was down there, she could only have fallen from this ledge.

Paula lay flat on the lip of the cave floor, peering down. 'Magda!' she called. 'Magda, what happened?'

But the dream was going through a scrambler again, and when Magda answered it was the voice of Angus once more, calling her own name.

Paula closed her eyes as a bitter liquid rose in her throat and dislodged the green thread into her mouth again. She beat on the rock floor with her fist and felt a chunk crumble off and fall away below. 'Angus!' she screamed, willing reality to finish and the dream take over forever.

Then there was more scrabbling on rock; small stones and grit showered on her shoulders and hair. 'Paula, don't move!' Angus commanded. 'We're nearly there. Hang on, love. I'll be with you any second now.'

So, she had willed it and won. It was marvellous that there was no sensation any more. Nothing left but her fantasy.

Angus. Comfort. Safety.

CHAPTER 17

It was no illusion that swept her hard into his arms a few moments later, but Angus in the flesh, solid and warm and squeezing her to death. Paula ground her forehead into his cheek, twisting her head from side to side in vehement denial of some unspoken accusation. She tried to speak and the words came out in a long-drawn moan. He went on holding her, stroking her hair gently, easing the sun-dried strands free of her blistered face. 'What was that you said, love?'

She tried again. 'Motherlove!' She choked on the word. 'Magda. That's all it was. She did it for her son, and then it all went wrong.'

He didn't answer, letting the thought run free until it was possible that he knew what Paula meant. It seemed then that Frau Toller must have arranged the kidnap, using Petitjean as middleman. 'Anything,' he said at last, 'no matter what or how good, becomes obscene when taken too far. She was sick, Paula. Motherlove maybe, but gone sick.'

He thought of the Stockholm Syndrome, the textbook situation where the prisoner and the gaoler grew close through shared suffering, taking on each other's pain. But had the older woman really ever conceived what she'd put Paula through?

'It's a hard world,' he whispered, holding her close. 'Always has been. When reality gets to be too much, people turn it off, make up their own truth.'

'Magda did that.'

'And you didn't. You managed to hold out.'

'Touch and go. You came along in time. Oh Angus, if you hadn't!'

'I wasn't on my own. I've got another of life's casualties waiting up on the top. You owe him a lot. It could be mutual.' He told her about Foden, of his son's death from drugs, and his own early retirement and drinking problem. 'When you're ready, let's go and say hullo to him again.'

Foden had gone back down the north side of the rock. They found him hunkered in the moonlight, on the point of exhaustion and—despite his part in their success—embarrassed at coming face to face with the girl they'd come to save. He and Kostas between them had loaded Frau Toller from the islet's far side and then circled back. She lay now covered with blankets, pallid under the burnt skin, her eyes closed. Foden shook his head over her and Angus held Paula back as she moved towards the woman. 'Let her rest. It was a bad fall.'

Paula, still in a state of naked emotion went straight to Foden with both arms outstretched. He pulled her to him and rocked her against his chest as a father might comfort a child freshly wakened from a nightmare. 'You're safe,' he said fiercely into her hair. 'You've been lucky, got a good man there.'

'Two, with you.' And at last she could smile.

He turned his face away then, so that she shouldn't smell the fumes of brandy off him.

They waded out together between shelving rocks, holding hands. Then Kostas lifted her aboard from their arms. She lay trembling on the slippery deck while he reached down his great bear-paws to heave the other two over the gunwales. She'd heard the engine gently throbbing as they came down the cliff, and now he got busy with the anchor chain, brusquely waving off their offers of help, and sent them all for'ard where Magda lay unconscious.

As the caïque slid out from under the lea they looked back to see the half moon come up over the shoulder of the rock that hid the cave. It lit a bright ladder over the lengthening sea between them and the islet. It exposed too their vulnerable faces and they turned away again all at the same moment, to gaze out ahead, eager for the first sighting of Crete's dark outline.

Kostas didn't feel happy at taking their money, but fuel was too expensive for him to indulge a taste for chivalry, and it was his brother's boat after all. In the end he satisfied his ursine sense of fitness by bringing from the cabin a flat basket piled with purple figs, insisting that they took it. The men gripped his hand on leaving. Paula reached up and kissed him, Greek fashion, on both cheeks, gripping his shoulders. He was dropping them near his brother's house, where the car was, and taking the injured woman on to hospital. Some official would have to go out for the body later.

'Mr Foden should remember the way,' he muttered, a grizzly to the last. 'Up the path ahead—*isseéa*—then there's an olive grove, some old buildings where no one live any more. Go past and turn right where the hippies camp once. When the path lead uphill, take the left fork. In ten minutes you are on the road to Mátala.'

'It's a bit of a climb,' Foden warned Paula. 'We could carry you between us.'

She shook her head. 'I'm wobbly, but sort of excited. I have to keep going.'

'Then I'll go ahead, try to stop a car on the road. If you're certain you're okay.'

'With Angus, I'll be fine. Really.'

'Yes, of course.' He groped in his back pocket and passed something hand-sized and flat to Angus. 'Look, take this. I kept some in case—but it wouldn't be advisable when she's been so empty. Just as an extreme measure, eh? It's Metaxa.'

Angus slid the hip flask in his own pocket and Foden nodded. 'Well, I'll be seeing you both, then. At the road if not before.' He went on alone along the twisting path. His stumbling footfalls faded to an indistinct scuffle, then died away. For Angus and Paula there was a private matter that had been put off too long. For a while they leaned together wordlessly and touched each other gently, but when they went on again they came upon Foden almost at once.

He stood silhouetted at the dark edge of a ruined building, one arm supporting him as he stared out into the moonlit clearing ringed by misshapen olive trees. Beyond him in the half-light they glimpsed slow, fluid movement. As Mott and the girl came up behind he was unaware of them, a watcher observed.

It was one of the boy dancers. Quite alone, isolated from reality, he was taking a bath in mime, dreamily in love with his own body. They watched, holding their breaths, as the slight figure lingered over the pretended disrobing, ran languid fingers over shoulders, breast, down over jutting hips, smoothing his flanks, in a world of self-enchantment. Eerily, in total silence, he rose on half-points and began slowly to pivot, torso lowered and one arm longingly out-stretched while the opposite leg moved smoothly up behind in counterbalance. Then he straightened, stepped forward and stood tall, reaching thin arms sensually up into an imagined shower of water. The cascade in his mind was almost visible to the watchers. He was totally fluid, trans-formed in his fantasy.

Softly Mott touched Foden on one arm and heard the man's pent breath expelled. He tried to move forward, staggered, covered his eyes with a hand. Paula came up beside him ready to help.

'It's all right. For a moment I thought . . . imagined . . .'

They moved together in a close formation across the open patch of moonlight, past the poised statue. For a brief instant Paula saw moonlight reflected in the dancer's wide eyes. But the boy saw nothing. No movement of theirs would have penetrated the world he was in.

She put her arm through Foden's, supporting him along. *His dead son*, she knew intuitively. For a moment Foden had entered the fantasy himself, met up with the boy he had lost. Lost him again as the enchantment released him.

They went on in silence, through the tangle of overgrown olives and out on to the side of the hill. There was no other car on the road before they came on Kostas's Citröen. Angus took the driver's seat and Paula got in behind. Foden looked up directly at the moon and there were snail-traces of tears on his lined cheeks. '"Whom the gods would destroy they first send mad." And there are many forms of madness.'

Angus knew then, being so near its agony himself, that Foden had emerged. Or perhaps was just on the verge, taking his first step forward into unaccustomed light, dazzled, still bemused, but coming free. Maybe, when they had all the hideous events sorted out and finally took their flight from Iraklion, there could be a third seat booked. For Foden, a man returning from the valley of the shadow.

Kostas had telephoned ahead as promised and in Iraklion arrangements had been made. At the hotel the Kápetan was waiting to question Angus, and a uniformed nurse had prepared Paula's room for a medical examination. There was one official photographer and a tape-player set to 're-cord', but before the police could approach Paula she had a check-up from a doctor, was fed soup and allowed to sleep undisturbed.

When she awoke it was Monday evening. The nurse was

still in attendance, but Paula insisted on getting up for her statement to the police. At its end, 'I'm going down to dinner,' she announced, 'but I haven't a thing to wear.'

Alerted to the problem, both Scott twins offered outfits of their own, but Paula quickly accepted the loan of a pale blue sheath dress from Melissa Bowles. It was a grand occasion, which the chef made much of. Paula might have been mobbed but for the Kápetan's making up the foursome with Angus and Foden. It kept others at bay.

While they ate, the Kápetan explained about Khalida, who had almost certainly caused little Sayid's death. They would never have understood his connection with Petitjean if the silly woman hadn't kept his letter sent to her in Belgium last autumn. It had been a *mésalliance* contracted when both were young, and physical attraction had out-weighed the differences of race and upbringing. There had been a child, a girl Tammam, whom the mother intended taking back to Belgium after her nursing contract expired in Lebanon. Khalida, however, whether from spite for his wife or real affection for the child, had beaten her to it, decamping and taking the baby Tammam with him. Nothing had been heard of them since. Irène had tried to trace them secretly, but would not own to having married a PLO man, unless there was some hope of having Tammam back. Now, after seventeen years, Tammam was presumably grown into a young woman and found a woman's life in Libya, where they'd fetched up, not to her taste. She'd begged her father to get her to Europe, and by then he had come to see that there her options would be wider. He had approached the mother to find the girl a safe place in the West. But Tammam couldn't get an exit permit because some powerful man in Tripoli had an alternative marked out for her.

'It was Petitjean who arranged your marooning,' said the Kápetan, 'not Frau Toller, although it suited her plans to make a match between you and her son. Petitjean drove you all to Mátala, collected Tammam from Skoufas who'd sailed out to take her off a Libyan boat, and I believe it was Petitjean who paid him to strand you while she got her daughter away in your place.'

'I was so sure that it was Magda's doing,' Paula admitted. 'You see, Skoufas wasn't just drunk. He'd been given something. I thought of Jozsef's tranquillizers, and that Magda had introduced a large dose into his food. I overlooked the *ouzo* from Irène. He was the only one drinking that. Of course, she was a nurse. She would have brought with her something like morphine or phenobarbitone.' She shuddered. 'I've never met anyone so cold-blooded. It didn't matter to her what became of us, or how many lives she destroyed, just to get her own ends, recover her daughter.'

Angus grunted. 'You were right about one thing. The villain of the piece *was* motherlove, the twisted sort.'

'Unfortunately,' the Kápetan said, 'she can never confirm all this for us, since she too has been killed. First stabbed and then pushed into the harbour, rather clumsily tied under an old boat.'

'By Khalida, to cover up his tracks?' Angus demanded.

'No, he'd meant to use her, and he hasn't yet returned to Crete. Tammam's line of communication is cut, with Skoufas being drowned, but she will find another way to summon him, and then we'll be there.'

'You have the girl?' Paula asked. 'Why didn't she leave on my passport as intended?'

The Kápetan chuckled. 'Because another girl beat her to it. The younger nurse, Sylvie Audoin, was terrified of her companion by then, sure some violence was intended against herself. She took the wig which Petitjean had bought for the purpose, and the stolen passport, and she flew off—as she thought—for London. And the next one marooned was Tammam, with no identity papers and no friends, because for some reason she and her mother were at daggers drawn. Literally so, because we have found the knife used to kill

Petitjean. With the same fingerprints as on a bottle of lemon juice handled by a certain customer in the store opposite the apartment where Frau Toller used to live. That is where Petitjean took Tammam in desperation when the original escape plan fell through. It was a temporary measure because she expected Frau Toller to return. But Petitjean was killed, and Tammam is still there, waiting for her father—who may not, perhaps, be her father at all, but her lover who played a clever doublecross to get her smuggled out of Libya through the least suspicious agent—his denounced Western wife.'

'So there are still loose ends,' said Angus thoughtfully. 'The Tammam–Khalida link, Frau Toller, and Sylvie Audoin.'

'I do not think,' the Kápetan said gently, 'that Frau Toller has much more to suffer in this life. Her injuries were severe when she fell down the cliff, and there is some concern about her heart. As for Tammam, we hourly expect her reunion with Zeid Khalida. And we have news from Brussels that the younger nurse, Audoin, has been sighted in her parents' village. There should shortly be a full report on her part in this business.'

Sylvie Audoin walked in her parents' small-holding and turned in her mind what she should do next. Getting back had not been all that difficult. She had abandoned the black wig at Frankfurt in a public toilet, sure that some woman would fancy it and cram it in her handbag. For herself she never wanted to see it again. The very thought of it made her sick.

She had used travellers' cheques for her fare on the Europabus, which was slow but anonymous, and she crossed into Belgium on her own papers. *I, Sylvie Audoin, being of sound mind* . . . but only just! No, that was for a Will Form, not a confession. Confession had another form of words, foreign to her because she was brought up strictly Protestant.

Confession was Catholic and so forbidden, but sometimes it must be so good to have.

She was feeding the hens, scattering handfuls of corn mixed with little lumps of stodge, and picking her way among their droppings, her nostrils offended by the long-remembered, long-rejected smell of their sweaty feathers. Across the yard she could see her father, shrivelled and stooping, fiddling in the old tractor's engine with a spanner. There were diagonal smears of black on his overalls seat where he always wiped his greasy hands. Her mother—her mother would be indoors, also shrivelled but not stooping. Rather, she was tightly drawn together, seeming to get more wasted and yellow every day, surely dying before their eyes but unable to acknowledge it herself. She was taking tablets for the pain, going on going on, her little, hard eyes defying them to deny she always would. Hard, yes hard. Hard on herself, hard on them. Always was.

This was the world she had come back to, the world she'd earlier escaped from—over the childhood years by immersing herself in schoolwork, and later in the difficult struggle for nursing qualifications and the licence it bestowed to follow a calling elsewhere. So she became a nurse and was free. Then she had woken up to there being another world beyond, which wasn't open to her. A world where others of her age belittled the things that totally filled her time and took all her energy to achieve, because for them it had been easy. Easy to pass exams, easy to mix with others, they had qualified, then set it all behind them, gone on to enjoy themselves. She was shamed by her own inability to do the same.

To them she was a background person, transparent, hardly there at all. It had made her angry, being so centred inside this person they didn't recognize. She longed for significance, for better qualifications, for status. She had decided that if she did not count it was because she was alone, had no friends, no husband. And started stupidly to dream of how it might be different. Well, see where it led. She was back where she had begun.

How they had stared when she walked in, with no luggage but a duffel bag, but they never questioned her breaking off a foreign holiday to come 'home'. It had been too hot, she'd said, and they could see the burnt state of her arms and legs. Nothing more of her showed, because here bikinis didn't exist. She wore a faded cotton overall she'd had in her later schooldays, and it still wasn't tight over her woman's breasts. That disturbed her a little, as the whole place did, making her aware of time having passed but of herself standing still, life escaping. What had made her like this, incapable of reaching out, incapable even of wanting anything strongly enough to decide to reach out?

I have my training, she told herself. I am a staff nurse. That is something. It excused her for not staying home to preserve the family trinity. (Georges, her older brother, had escaped to a wife, even had his own small stretch of land to work.) Being a nurse hadn't been quite enough, though. Hence the crazy notion Sister Petitjean had come up with, making her think she could find romance on a holiday. Romance, and even the chance of becoming some substantial man's wife.

Well, it wasn't for her. She knew now. When her holiday leave was over she'd do better to slot back in hospital routine where she belonged. As her parents belonged here. She would, in a way, be like her mother—going on going on. Until she stopped. The alternative was too alarming. Meeting men outside duty, trying to open up, talking to them and knowing all the time that behind the words they were thinking about—well, *that*. Having you. It was easier not to make the effort, keep apart, just accept the sun and the meals and the scenery. On her own. Sex, well she didn't need men. She'd manage on her own, as she'd always done. Safer that way.

But the fear hadn't all come from that direction. She

could see much clearer now, with distance, that it was Irène she'd been scared of. Irène, so helpful at first, full of ideas, planning the project, encouraging her when she lost heart. Joking, calling herself a marriage-broker. Then, when Sylvie began to see it was a mistake, standing back with something like contempt. And so busy still with plans, a *ruthless* woman —but what was she really up to? She hadn't just been helping Sylvie out. There was much more behind all her unaccountable comings and goings from the hotel. And the night that little Egyptian boy had fallen and been killed Irène had been out of their room. The phone had rung after they were in bed, and while Sylvie pretended to be asleep, Irène had put on a dressing-gown and gone out. There had been the soft sound of the lift opposite their door and about twenty minutes later the same sound again before Irène stole back. She wouldn't have gone down to the public rooms in pyjamas and dressing-gown, and they had their own bathroom. That left someone else's room or the roof. It was from the roof that the boy had fallen.

From then on, Sylvie had watched her, trying not to show that she did, because she was afraid of this new Irène who added deceit to her undoubted efficiency. She was plotting with an unknown person, doing unaccountable things that involved phone calls and sudden solo shopping. When she was out, Sylvie had gone through her cases and found the black wig, a hypodermic syringe and ampoules. The labels on them showed they were insulin, but they weren't the original hospital labels. They were substitutes, handwritten. If Irène had been diabetic Sylvie would have known from what she ate, could have given the injections. In any case there were only three doses, never enough for another nine or ten days. So perhaps it wasn't insulin at all, but just labelled that in case the luggage was searched en route.

All of which made her more frightened, and so more suspicious. Then she found the screwed up paper in the waste bin and discovered Irène's list of things to do, a sort of shorthand timetable with scratchings out and reversed sequences of some sinister-seeming plan. The overall purpose wasn't clear, but enough of it had Sylvie frantic with fear. 'Emetic for S' certainly applied to herself on the day before she was to go on Frau Toller's drive to the south. She was violently sick after dinner and three times in the night. By morning she'd felt like death and was pleased to have the English girl take her place while she stayed in bed.

Just before Irène was to leave with the Hungarians she had run back to their room. Lying in bed, Sylvie had watched in the mirror as she hid something in her undies drawer. As soon as she was alone Sylvie had gone to look. There was an extra passport, with a blue cover. The name and the photograph inside were Paula Musto's.

Sylvie had meant to warn her that night when she returned, but it had to be in secret for fear of Irène, who was now revealed as some kind of evil-doer. Sylvie had been taught about evil from her childhood, but in between had somehow forgotten the warnings. Now it all came back in the voice of the preacher: the Evil that Walketh by Night to Destroy Man; Corruption that Puts Forth its Hand to Foul with its Touch; Possession by Devils.

Sick with apprehension, she had taken Paula's key from the board in the foyer when Reception was empty, and had gone up to hide in the English girl's room, taking with her the wig and the stolen passport. She would have taken the little box with the syringe and ampoules too but it had gone. Irène had taken it with her.

It grew late and Paula didn't come, but Sylvie was too frightened to go back to the room she shared with Irène. Let her worry a little. She would never think to look for Sylvie here.

She slept and woke and slept again. Some time during the night she just knew that Paula wasn't coming back. There would be no one to tell about Irène's mad wickedness. And after Paula it was herself that Irène would turn upon.

She thought desperately about escape, and the packed cases showed her the way out. She had only to add to them Paula's toilet things, nightdress and the trouser suit still in the wardrobe, then put them out in the corridor for collection. This was the day Paula would leave, going home to London. She had Paula's passport and a wig enough like her hair to satisfy Immigration control. She could get away herself, reach London by afternoon, catch the next available plane for Brussels out of Heathrow. All she needed was to keep her head down when any of the Fiesta group were near. On the coach and at the airport she'd keep right away.

There had been scaring moments on the journey: the flight interrupted at Frankfurt, and the necessary stopover; that wretched man who had tried to make love to her. She'd only talked to him because he fetched her boarding card and it kept the others away. Then she'd thought the Canadian woman would recognize her when they collided in the Airbus aisle, and a second time at the Frankfurt hotel. The telegram from some friend of Paula's in London had put her off continuing to Heathrow. Instead it had been so simple to become herself again and come straight here. It didn't matter that her holiday luggage was still in Crete.

It was strange having been someone else. Not altogether unpleasant. Freer than this, gone back to the restraints of childhood. She felt that left here she would suffocate before long. She was not sure that return to the hospital would be much better. How could she ever face Irène Petitjean again, both knowing what they did about each other?

The fear tightened about her once more and pain returned behind her eyes. As she came slowly round the corner of the house she saw the little police car at the front gate and two *agents* walking towards her. She stopped, then went mechanically forward again, almost relieved. It was going to be taken out of her hands. She would not have to make any decisions.

The foremost one was very neat with shiny pink skin,

middle-aged, quite ordinary. He looked like someone you could talk to.

CHAPTER 18

Paula had the faintest of smiles on her lips when she left the dining-room with Angus. At the terrace steps she pulled a flower from the bougainvillæa that hung over the wall. Her voice sounded puzzled. 'I found your tie, and two shirts. In my wardrobe.'

'I've been using your room.'

'Ah. And last night?'

'They found me somewhere else.' He sounded martyred. 'A broom cupboard. A matchbox.'

'Poor love.' Her eyes were teasing him.

'So, can I move back?'

'I think that would be—very cosy.'

'Good.' He put an arm round her. 'Now that I've got through to the middle of the labyrinth I'm not risking losing sight of you again. What shall we do tomorrow while the Kápetan's men are beavering away to get everything ready for us to sign?'

'Ask Kostas for his car again. Say our goodbyes to Crete.'

Later, in their room, she told Angus, 'I've been talking to Keith Foden.' She stopped brushing her hair to grimace in the mirror at the patchwork healing of her skin.

'He's trying to dry out. Am I right?'

'Sort of. But he's not a real alcoholic, so I don't think he has to cut it out entirely. Just modify. Drinking was only a symptom of his not being able to take life's hard edges. Now he feels back in it, recuperative anyway. He's decided to move on.'

'Leave the island?'

'He's going to the mainland as a first stage. London's too

complicated for him yet. I asked the Kápetan to wangle us *three* tickets to Athens. And I pulled strings, through the Antoniades Corporation, to reserve him a good room at the Electra Palace. It's central and he wants to try out city life.'

Angus regarded her thoughtfully. 'Electra Palace rings a bell. That's where your Van Leidens are staying. Paula, you're matchmaking.'

'Not exactly. Just placing them near enough to see if anything comes of it. They all need somebody. There's been so much tragedy, I'd like some good to come out—'

He saw her eyes were brimming. 'My poor love, it's been hell for you. Come and let me cuddle you up.'

They lay and whispered together in the dark while the night sounds of Iraklion came distantly through the balcony shutters: a bell tolling eleven strokes, the low hum of traffic, neighbours calling softly from rooftop to rooftop below, *bouzouki* music and faint bursts of applause or laughter.

'I wonder,' Paula said sleepily, 'what's happened to the Kápetan?' At dinner she had been explaining to the others how Petitjean had excused herself at the last moment from the island picnic. Irène had gone to check by telephone that Sylvie was recovering from her sickness, and came back to say she was worse and needing an immediate operation for appendicitis. She just had to be there when Sylvie came round. So she had taken the hire car back and the others had agreed to return by taxi or long distance bus after the picnic. No one doubted the truth of her story.

'When I began to suspect the marooning was deliberate,' Paula explained, 'I blamed Frau Toller in my mind. I thought she was more than a little mad. But she wasn't then, not until Jozsef died. Then she couldn't accept it. He'd been her whole future. She's not the sort to break down herself, so she broke with reality instead. I can't feel sorry for Irène when I think what misery she caused without a second's thought. Even Skoufas hadn't deserved such a dreadful end.'

Then while the Kápetan enumerated Skoufas's known villainies, a messenger had made his way between the tables to summon his chief to the final act of the drama. He had grimaced with disgust and thrown down his napkin. '*Méringue Chantilly*, and Khalida has to be sighted now!'

'We'll keep it for you,' Paula promised.

'Confound the man, no! Khalida can wait. If he runs true to form he won't approach direct. He likes to throw pursuers off, even when they don't exist. We'll wait for him near the girl, who's much less experienced.' He finished his dessert and patted his paunch. 'Now I am fortified. I can go and be fierce.'

Out in the waiting car he had exchanged his uniform jacket for a pale linen coat and sat in the rear, lighting a big cigar, playing the leisured plutocrat relaxing between engagements. The car rolled towards the harbour area and parked a little short of the Toller apartment on the opposite side. The radio came suddenly alive. 'Approaching the building's rear. Subject going in.'

The Kápetan flicked a switch on his hand set. 'Cyclops to Pollux. Give them eight minutes, recording all speech. I'm coming across.' He opened the car door, stretched himself, glanced casually around and strolled diagonally across the street, past the Toller entrance. In the lea of the building he came back, pushed open the unlatched door and went softly upstairs. On the landing his lieutenant was frowning at his watch. The listening devices were in place on the wall.

The lieutenant looked up, the Kápetan nodded, stepped back and kicked. The door went in.

At eleven-fifty the phone rang in Paula's room and Angus reached for it, instantly alert.

'It was as I supposed,' the Kápetan's fat chuckle told him. 'Khalida was anything but the girl's father. He had hoped to cut free from his past and start afresh elsewhere with her. No more killings, no more bombs. So he said. The real Tammam died as quite a small child, in the care of his sister. This one's a tigress. We hold her for the murder of Petitjean who discovered the truth because the girl's a bad actress and taunted her a little too soon. There was an almighty row when Petitjean failed to produce the wig and passport for her journey as promised. It reinforced the suspicions roused by the change from Khalida's original plan. Both women flew at each other, but the Libyan was the one with the knife. Impetuous, she'll come apart easily when we question her in depth. Khalida—well, he has killed many in his time, and is wanted in at least three countries, but we shall get him for young Sayid. Of course, he will try to buy us off with some valuable information about his fellow terrorists.'

The Kápetan snarled. 'A jackal, that man.' Then he laughed. Angus could picture the curved, yellow teeth. 'But *we* are the vultures; we eat first.'

Angus laid down the receiver. 'He's got them both. It's all over. Now you can sleep.'

Goodbyes were said at the hotel. Even Andy Whitelaw abandoned his office work to see them off in the private car driven by the Kápetan himself. Foden sat beside him looking unusually pale but correct, dimly the Senior Civil Servant. Suddenly, in the back seat, Angus sat bolt upright. 'Who was K?' he demanded of Paula. 'The one in your diary.'

Paula was mystified until he quoted, '*Goodbye drinks at K's.*'

Foden interrupted. 'I worked that one out. Elsewhere in the diary Paula shortened place-names to the first and last letter. It was the apostrophe S that fooled us. Not possessive at all. M'a for Mátala, I'n for Iraklion, so *K's*—'

'For Knossos,' Angus muttered. 'Goodbye drinks at Knossos.'

'Which we had,' Paula said. 'You and I, at the *taverna* by

the entrance. Originally I'd meant to throw a little party.'

'The big mystery,' Angus marvelled. 'The simplest solution.'

'I'll get three coffees in the departure lounge,' Foden offered when the luggage had gone off.

The Kápetan said goodbye briskly. 'We need you all again for the trial. Could you return—at the time of the wine-tasting?' His eyes disappeared in fleshy cheeks as he laughed, turning away.

'He's quite human, when you know him,' Paula marvelled.

'A damn good copper. Look, love, I have to go and ring Chichester, find out how far Barry and Angie have taken the boat. Do I say we're coming, or have you had enough of the sea?'

Paula smiled. It was still painful, but the doctor's cream was healing the cracked skin. She had wound her dark hair on top of her head with a silver comb and it shone now with coconut oil. 'Of course we go sailing. I've discovered my seamanship needs working on. And if we get anywhere near Jersey we'll look in on Mother. It's time you both met. Go and ring Barry. Tell them I'm sorry I upset the arrangements.'

She waited while he was connected with Chichester and was given a second number to try. After a further delay she saw him talking animatedly, grinning his wide, slice-of-melon smile. When he came away from the phone there was a whimsical quirk to his eyebrows.

'Well?'

'I passed on your apologies, explained in short that you'd run aground. They're very forgiving, quite understand it's a thing that happens. Barry said—' Angus's smile broadened as he slid his arm round her shoulders—'he's glad it was nothing serious!'

THE END